A MISSING SURFER.

AN ABANDONED MANSION.

A DEADLY SECRET...

When a surfer disappears near one of the creepiest beach-front mansions in Crescent Bay, the Digital Detectives stumble onto their next big mystery. The house once belonged to an eccentric scientist, Tibias Mandrake, who performed some very bizarre experiments in his laboratory. But now that the house is on the real estate market, some people in Crescent Bay are dying to get their hands on it....

To solve the mystery, you'll make on-line investigations of the mansion, a pitch-black cave, and Mandrake's secret lab. Analyze every fingerprint, interrogate every suspect, and record everything in your on-line crime journal. Remember: if you miss a single clue, you might not live to solve another case!

DIGITAL DETECTIVES MYSTERIES

MYSTERIES

WHEN NIGHTMARES COME TRUE

by Jay Montavon

RUNNING PRESS
Philadelphia · London

9   8   7   6   5   4   3   2   1
Digit on the right indicates the number of this printing

Library of Congress Cataloging-in-Publication Number 00-133410

ISBN 0-7624-0906-1

Digital Detectives™ developed by enhanceNOW.com, Carla Jablonski,
and Jay Leibold

Designed by Bill Jones
Cover illustrations © 2000 by Mike Harper
Series Editor: Carla Jablonski
Running Press Editors: Jason Rekulak and Susan Hom
enhanceNOW Editor: Jason Zietz
Typography: Minion, Futura, and Orbital

This book may be ordered by mail from the publisher.
Please include $2.50 for postage and handling.
But try your bookstore first!

Running Press Book Publishers
125 South Twenty-second Street
Philadelphia, Pennsylvania 19103-4399

Visit us on the web!
www.runningpress.com

CHAPTERS

WELCOME, DIGITAL DETECTIVE!

The first time you log on to the Digital Detectives web site,

http://www.ddmysteries.com

you will be required to choose a user name. Once you have received your user name, write it in the space below.

_____

Digital Detective User Name

Your user name will bookmark your investigative work on the web site, so that you can continue where you left off.

WARNING:

This is _not_ a typical mystery. You _should not_ read every page of this book—that would spoil many of the story's best surprises! You will be directed on-line at certain points to gather evidence from the crime scenes. The web site will tell you which page of this book to return to. Do a good job, and you'll solve the crime! Make a sloppy investigation and... well, some _very_ bad things can happen...

Good luck!

1
THE DANGERS OF SLEEP

You wake with a start. Flames dance all around you. They lick at the house, ready to consume you. You throw off your bed covers, leap to your feet, and test the door to your room.

It's cool to the touch, not hot as it would be if there were a fire outside. A moment later, as you come awake, you realize there are no flames. The heat is coming from your own body. Your pajamas are soaked with sweat. Suddenly, the night air feels good on your wet skin.

You press your hands against the door again, inhaling deeply. You detect a faint odor of smoke, but it doesn't seem to be coming from nearby.

You open the door a crack. It is comfortingly dim in the hallway—not ablaze, as you were sure it had been just moments ago. A little plug-in night light gives off a tender glow.

But the dream was so real, you have to check the rest of the house to be certain. You start down the hall. The door to your little sister Eve's room is ajar. You peek in. She's safe and sound.

The door to your parents' room is wide open. The room is empty, as you expect. They are out of town for a week at a conference.

You creep down the stairs. Behind the door of the guest room is your mother's cousin, Candace, asleep. Nothing

1

wakes her. Telephones, doorbells, barking dogs—she snoozes through them all. If anyone is going to watch out for the safety of your house in the dead of night, it will have to be you.

The living room, kitchen, and garage are all dark and quiet. Finally, you allow yourself a sigh of relief. There is no fire, after all. You get yourself a glass of water from the kitchen and start back up the stairs.

Then you stop and glance down at the front door. What if the fire is outside? Better check.

You go back down the stairs and unhook the door latch. You turn the lock, then the knob, and slowly crack open the door. Cool October air pours over your skin. You step out to the porch.

The night is illuminated by a half moon. The dark ribbon of street is empty. A breeze ruffles the dry leaves in the trees. You shiver in your sweaty pajamas.

You draw in a deep breath, and now you can smell it. The smoke. It's been lingering over your town of Crescent Bay for the past couple of days. Autumn is fire season in northern California. A wildfire has been raging in the coastal mountains to the east. The town is safe, but when the wind shifts to the west, the smoke tingles in your throat.

The breeze drops for a moment, allowing you to hear the faint roar of the Pacific Ocean in the distance. You smile when you hear an especially big crash. The waves are still big. You've had some good days surfing with your friends Randy and Tina lately. From what you're hearing, you'll have another good day after school tomorrow.

The thought cheers you, and you turn to go back inside, finally ready for sleep again.

* * *

"I had the dream again last night," you tell Satellite Jack at the beach the next day.

Jack is settling himself into his blue-striped folding chair. He works the frame of the chair into the sand until it's stable. Then he pulls the little canopy attached to the back of the chair over his head, shading himself and the briefcase on his lap.

"Hmm," Jack responds, opening the briefcase. Inside is a high-powered laptop computer.

You, Randy and Tina are here at the shore to surf the waves of the Pacific. Jack will do all his surfing from his beach chair, courtesy of a wireless connection to the World Wide Web.

"It's the second night in a row," you add. "The flames crackle and roar around me. Or they're laughing at me. I jump out of bed and my skin's really hot—"

"Are you sick?" Jack asks. "Have a temperature?"

"No, I feel fine."

He squints up at you through his round glasses and purses his lips. "Maybe it's the smoke from that fire on the other side of the mountains. You smell the smoke while you're asleep, which sets off an alarm in your brain. It thinks there's a fire nearby. But since you're asleep, you can't tell your brain to ignore it."

"Hmmm." His explanation makes sense.

You regard Jack's doughy face, unmarked by sun, as he starts to tap on the computer with his pudgy fingers. It's beyond you how a kid his age—13, same as you—can be so smart.

But you've gotten used to it by now.

You met Jack, Tina, and Randy when you moved to Crescent Bay this summer. Randy lives on your block, so he was the first one you met. At the beginning, you were happy that Randy would even talk to you. He's a year older, dark-haired, athletic—star forward on the soccer team—and respected by everyone. But as you got to know him, you found out that he was even nicer than that. He's a guy who values his friends—good, loyal, honest friends—more than anything.

Maybe that's what draws all four of you together. While you have something in common with each of your three friends, Tina, Randy, and Jack seemed an unlikely group at first glance.

Tina is a daredevil. When you picture her, it's on skateboard, green eyes alight, red hair flying in the wind, a big smile showing her chipped front tooth. On the other hand, when you think of Jack, you see him enchanted by a screen full of computer code, or tinkering with his latest piece of headgear. He has invented gadgets that allow him to listen in on a conversation twenty yards away and download a new piece of music from the Web at the same time.

Jack and Tina have known each other since kindergarten, so that sort of explains why they're so comfortable with each other. But there's something more, something in the chemistry between the four of you that's a kind of magic.

The magic took a concrete form when you banded together last month to become the Digital Detectives. You had stumbled on a computer game piracy ring, which turned out to be a cover for something even more sinister: a computer virus that was eating kids' hard drives. Together you succeeded in solving the crime and getting the culprit put behind bars. Everyone was amazed that you were able to crack the case. But Jack's smarts—not to mention the ingenious high-tech devices he's invented—together with Tina's boldness and Randy's good sense made for a good team. You're the one who was able to put it all together.

Now, at the beach, you're jolted out of your thoughts by a hand clapping you on the shoulder.

"So why are we standing around on dry land when there are some tasty curls out there?"

It's Randy, grinning his it's-a-gorgeous-day-and-the-surf-is-going-off grin. Tina's right behind him. Like you, they're wearing neoprene and rubber wetsuits for insulation from the frigid northern California water.

Surf culture in Crescent Bay is not how you'd imagined it. This is not southern California, with its baking sand, mild waves, jams and bikinis. Most of the currents in northern California come straight from Alaska. No matter what time of year you go out, a session in the water is like a bracing slap of winter. Being originally from Colorado, you love it.

"Be careful out there," Jack advises, as you head toward the water with Tina and Randy. It's a little ritual of his. He won't let you go in until he's said it.

"You know it," you promise Jack the way you always do. You grab your board and dash for the waves. Dashing right along with you is Randy's dog Joe. Joe is a black cocker spaniel with the most human face you've ever seen. On warm days like today, Joe will bound right into the water with you.

The icy salt water feels good as you splash into it. You jump on your board and begin to paddle. Joe's right there, swimming beside you. Randy puts Joe on his board. They float around together; Joe taking in all the sights from his perch.

A big wave rises up and crashes in front of you. You push down hard on your board to duck under the oncoming churn. When it hits, your sinuses get thoroughly reamed with salt water. This was something you didn't like at all about surfing when you first started. But now you almost look forward to the taste of the sea in the back of your throat.

Once the wave is past, you paddle like crazy to get out past the next incoming breaker before it crushes you. This is called getting "outside"—beyond the point where the waves are curling and crashing. Once there, you find relative calm.

You relax on your board for a minute and feel the steady rhythm of the swells, one after another. Tina joins you. You ask where Randy is.

"He took Joe back to shore," she says. "That one big wave knocked him off Randy's board."

"Guess Joe didn't keep his head up," you remark.

Tina laughs. "Right, he wasn't following the advice of his master."

Randy always says that life is a lot like surfing. There's always going to be a wave coming at you. Sometimes they crush you, and sometimes they give you the ride of your life. Either way, you have to keep your head up and watch for the next one.

Together you and Tina gaze out at the water. The sun is already low. It's late October, and the days are getting short. The sky is a hazy orange. The sun is dimmed by the lingering smoke of the wildfire. The smoke also makes the salt water sting your throat a little more than usual.

Tina sits up, straddling her board, and looks out to the horizon. You can't sit up because you're on a bodyboard, which is smaller than a surfboard. Sometimes it's called a "sponge" because of the material it's made of, and sometimes "toast," because of its shape. You found it easier to get acquainted with the ocean by starting on the bodyboard, but one day you'll try a surfboard.

"Here comes one," Tina says.

You turn and see a nicely shaped wave steaming your way. You kick and paddle hard to catch it. With a couple of graceful paddles, Tina pulls even with you. The wave jacks up. You feel air being sucked into its hollow curl. You're sucked into it as well, and then everything happens very quickly. In a flash, you're at the top of the curling wave. You see Tina spring to her feet. She zips down into the wave, as if she has rocket engines on her surfboard. You crank your board to the left as well, and all of a sudden you're slicing across the glassy face of the wave, as it roars all around you. It only lasts for a few seconds, yet it feels like forever that you're suspended there.

Then the wave crashes and you're cruising on white foam. You pull out of it before it takes you too far toward shore. There's Tina, bobbing beside her surfboard, a giant grin on her face.

Randy pulls up to you. "Not bad," he says.

"Awesome," Tina corrects him, delirious from her ride.

"Ready to paddle out for another set?" Randy asks.

"Of course!"

You catch a few more waves, and miss a few too, as the sun sinks to the horizon. Happily, you avoid any major disasters, which at this point in your surfing career you are always thankful to do.

Most of the other surfers have already gone in. You wait with Tina and Randy for one last wave. Suddenly, Randy, sitting on his board, points to something in the ocean. "Hey, what's that over there—does that look like a surfer to you?"

He's pointing at the rough waters on the jagged coast just north of you. You're surfing at the top end of Crescent Bay's crescent. The waves from the northwest hook around a rocky point before coming into the bay. Above the point, the land rises to a steep, wild bluff. The shore itself is nearly impassable, and rock formations, called haystacks, dot the water off the coast, making navigation treacherous.

You push yourself up on your board to get a look. But you can't raise yourself high enough. Tina is sitting on her board, though, and she spots him.

"Yeah," she says. "It looks like a surfer to me. He's got blond hair, I think."

"It's a guy on a board all right," Randy confirms, leaning forward. "He's not paddling or anything. He's just lying there."

"Maybe he fell asleep," you suggest.

"Whatever it is, he's drifting into a really dangerous place," Randy says. "All it would take is one decent-size wave to smash him up against the rocks. What is he *doing* out there?"

"He might need help," Tina says. "Let's go in."

The three of you catch the next wave to shore. Jack looks concerned when he sees you running toward him.

"Call search-and-rescue," Randy instructs him. "There's a surfer lost out there. He's drifting up toward the bluff. Tina, maybe you can call your dad, too."

Then Randy plucks at your wetsuit. "Come on, let's try to

keep him in sight. The tide is low and we can run up the shore." He turns back to Tina and Jack. "We'll meet you guys back here in half an hour."

You and Randy leave your board with Jack and dash off to look for the surfer.

2
DEVIL'S RACK

The beach ends at the top of Crescent Bay. From here on, the coastline turns rough and rocky. It's possible to pick your way up the shore, among boulders and over stone slabs and through tidepools, at low tide. But low tide lasts for only a little while. And you still have to watch for sneaker waves that can come up and smash you against the craggy wall of the bluff.

It doesn't help that you and Randy are still in your wetsuits, with only neoprene booties to protect your feet. But Joe, who is trotting along beside you, doesn't seem to have any problems. He stops and sniffs an occasional piece of kelp, then comes prancing after you, his ears bouncing eagerly.

You haven't caught sight of the missing surfer since you began your search. Already you've come half a mile up the coastline. You and Randy call out every few minutes. You jump up on a boulder to scan the sea.

"He couldn't have gone under…could he?" you ask with a shudder.

"Anything can happen here," Randy answers. "Do you know what they call this area? Devil's Rack. There's a little cove, a mile up the coast, where smugglers used to bring in moonshine from Canada. They're the ones who gave it the name. All these rock haystacks off shore looked like the knobs of a rack to them. They'd say, 'Don't get hung up on the Devil's Rack.'"

"Good advice," you mutter, squinting into the dimness ahead. The sun has disappeared. As the light fades, the stone shapes around you start to loom ominously, like giant creatures waiting to spring. The crashing surf seems louder and more ominous, too, as it turns into an invisible force shrouded by dusk.

"Yeah," Randy agrees. "We should get out of here. The tide is rising."

You've come to a small inlet. A creek has cut a wedge into the wall of the bluff. The water trickles down a steep slope. Something on the other side of the inlet catches your eye.

You grab Randy's arm. "Look at that. Up there, on top of the bluff."

"A light," Randy confirms.

It's coming from a dark shape towering from a promontory on the bluff. The shape almost seems to be part of the rock.

"That's the Mandrake house," Randy muses. "But wait a minute…he died a long time ago. My mom is trying to preserve it as a historic landmark. No one has lived there for years."

"Well, someone's there now," you say.

There's a pause between the breakers, and suddenly the world seems strangely silent. Then it dawns on you why.

"Where's Joe?" you ask. You don't hear the jingle of his tags.

"Joe!" Randy calls, a tinge of panic in his voice. "Joe!"

You hear a faint tinkle from the slope ahead of you. "There he is," you say. You point to a spot about a third of the way up the wall of the bluff.

"What are you doing there, Joe?" Randy scolds. Where the inlet has cut into the bluff, the walls rising to the top are not quite as steep as elsewhere. Joe has found a small footpath that climbs the slope. You follow it up to join him.

"Good idea, Joe," Randy says, patting the dog. He turns to you. "Let's go back this way. If this takes us to the top, I know a trail that we can take along the bluff to get back to the beach. It'll be safer than going back across the rocks."

"It's too dark to see the surfer anyway," you agree. You wonder if his broken, battered body is lying down there on the rocks, someplace where you missed it. Who was he? What was he doing out there?

Joe starts up the trail, and you and Randy follow. You're getting warm in your wetsuit, so you peel off the top and let it hang down over your waist. The trail zigzags up the steep, crumbly slope, past washed-out gullies and clumps of this-tle bush.

As you come around a bend of the trail, the house on the promontory comes into view again. It's much closer this time. Most of it is a dark, hulking mass, but one window is lit up like a star on a Christmas tree.

"Hey!" You spot a shadowy figure in the window. It appears to be hunched over and moving with great difficulty. You grab Randy and point to it. But the figure has already vanished.

"What is it?" Randy asks.

"There was someone up in that window," you say. "I wonder what's going on?"

"I don't know," Randy replies slowly. "Let's take a look."

You reach the top of the hundred-foot bluff, breathing

hard. Making your way through the fragrant coastal bushes, you approach the building from the left side. A tall iron fence encloses the mansion and its grounds. Joe finds a place where one iron bar is missing in the fence. You and Randy wriggle through after him.

You give a low whistle. "Whoa," you murmur.

The Mandrake house must have been quite an estate in its time. With the shred of light that's left, you see that the back of the mansion is perched directly over the Pacific Ocean. The front faces a huge lawn and formal garden. Now it is overgrown and fallen into disrepair. Someone has dug holes all over it. Vines climb up the brick walls of the house and obscure most of the ground floor windows. A tree lies dead and decaying in the middle of the lawn.

As you look closer, you realize there's something seriously strange about the house. At first glance, you thought it was a standard-issue dark brick mansion. But now you notice that all the angles are odd. None of them are square corners, instead they're either acute or obtuse. The windows are shaped like trapezoids. Even the walls don't rise straight up, but lean ominously over the onlooker.

"Weird place," Randy comments. "Let's find out who's in there. Maybe they saw what happened to the surfer."

"I don't know…" you reply.

"Let's just knock," Randy insists. "We owe it to the surfer."

You circle to the front and mount the steps to the door. This side of the house is completely dark. The windows, not covered by vines, stare back at you like blank eye sockets.

Randy pushes the doorbell button. It makes no sound. There's a giant knocker in the shape of what appears to be a thigh bone on the door. Randy uses it gingerly. You wait and listen, but hear nothing except the crashing surf below. He tries the doorknob, but the door is locked.

Randy knocks again. Nothing happens, but you notice that Joe is shrinking in fear against Randy's leg.

"Uh, Randy?" you begin. But your voice is cut off by an unholy shrieking that pierces the night. It's not one voice but many, rising and quavering on the night air, moaning and keening in high-pitched tones. Joe's legs are shaking. So are yours.

"Coyotes," Randy says.

"They sound so *miserable*," you say.

Randy chuckles and leans down to scratch his dog behind the ears. "Don't worry, Joe, I won't let them get you."

"I guess we better go back," you say.

"Yeah, Tina and Jack will be waiting for us."

Randy picks up Joe and carries him back to the break in the fence. You slip through and walk briskly away from the house. Behind you, you hear another unearthly howl. This time, it sounds like laughter.

* * *

"It's about time!" Jack says, after you've followed a shaggy, rutted trail across the bluff back to the beach. "We were about to send the search party out after you."

"Did you hear anything about the surfer?" you ask.

"Nope," Jack says. He's still in his beach chair. "We called it in, but haven't heard any more."

"I'll ask my dad when I get home," Tina says. Her father is a paramedic who works a lot with the sheriff and with rescue operations. "So where were you?"

15

"We walked along the shore at first," Randy answers. "Then Joe found this little trail that went up on the bluff."

"Cool," Tina says. "Isn't it kind of wild up there?"

"Wild doesn't begin to describe it," you remark.

"Joe would agree with you." Randy laughs and reaches down to pet his dog. "Kinda spooky up there, eh boy?"

"All I can say," you comment, "is that they gave Devil's Rack the right name."

"We went to this house," Randy says. "The abandoned one up there, the big mansion."

"Ooh, you mean the one on the cliff where that weird guy lives?" Tina says. "What's his name...Titus? We were told never to go out there."

"Tibias Mandrake," Randy replies. "And he's dead, as of a few years ago. My mom is trying to preserve the house as a historic landmark. Do you know anything about him, Jack?"

Jack shrugs. "Yeah, he was supposed to be some kind of genius who went sort of..." He makes circles by his ear. "You know, crazy."

"Well, we saw a light on in second floor of the house," you announce.

Tina's eyes bulge. *Really?*

"Yeah, and I saw someone in the window. Kind of a hunched person."

"Which is weird," Randy says, "because supposedly no one was ever found to inherit the house. That's why it's been empty for so long."

Jack strokes a pretend beard on his chin and says, "I smell a mystery."

"For sure," Tina agrees. "Call out the Digital Detectives."

Jack frowns. "I was kidding. I'm sure there's a logical—and

boring—explanation."

"I'm going to check with my mom," Randy says. "She'll know if there's supposed to be someone there."

You and Randy have been changing out of your wetsuits while you talk. Now you've got everything packed up. Jack folds his chair. The rest of you pick up your boards and start to walk back home. A half moon has made its way above the horizon to give you a little light.

You reach your house first. Saying goodbye to the others, you add, "I'll call you later. Or e-mail."

"Yeah, wait til you check your mail," Jack remarks. "Tina's been spamming us."

Tina pretends to swing her surfboard at Jack. "Cut it out. It could be for real."

"What? What is it?" you ask.

"You'll see," is all Tina will tell you.

* * *

Your little sister Eve and your mother's cousin, Candace, are reading a book on the sofa when you come in. Candace pauses to tuck a strand of streaked hair behind her ear. "Where have you been? It's kind of late."

"Surfing," you answer. "This surfer was drifting out to sea, and we went looking for him."

She frowns. "I hope he's all right. I left your dinner in the oven. You might need to microwave it for a minute."

"I ate all the dessert," Eve declares, scrunching her face into an impish grin.

You make an exaggerated growl at her. "Then I'm going to come and get it back out of you!"

Eve giggles and you go into the kitchen to get your dinner. Actually, you're kind of glad Candace asked where you were. She never worries too much about what you're up to. Usually you think that's just great, but sometimes you wish she'd show a little more concern. What if *you'd* been the lost surfer? How long would it take her to send a rescue party out after you?

You bring your dinner into the living room and listen to Candace read the story to Eve. When you finish eating, you announce that you're going up to your room.

"No, stay here," Eve pleads.

You mess up her hair. "I'll come back down later. I've got to check my e-mail and do some homework."

You leave your plate in the kitchen and go upstairs. Sitting at your desk, you stare out the dark window of your room. There's something lonely about this time of year. The early darkness closing in around the house; the chill that comes into the air at night; winter lurking.

You hate to admit it, but the house feels empty with your parents gone. Candace doesn't like TV, so not only is it empty, but quiet. Sometimes you like that, because it gives you a chance to think. But just now, you wish you could think of something that would warm you up and make the house feel cozy. Maybe Candace will let you have a fire in the fireplace. You dismiss the idea quickly, as you remember your dream from last night.

You reach over and turn on your computer. It whirrs to life in its cold, electronic way. You log on to your Internet account to pick up your e-mail. A headline on the site reminds you that daylight savings time will end this weekend. Great, you think; it'll get dark even earlier.

You find the message that Menace2U—that's Tina—has forwarded. Its subject line commands, DO NOT DELETE. It was originally sent by someone named Mordar.

Ignore or delete this message at your own peril.

You must send this message to 13 of your friends. If you do not, something terrible will happen to you within four days.

If you do not believe me, this is what happened to the people who ignored it. A girl in Poland was kidnapped. A man in London got a brain tumor. A family in Florida died in a head-on collision with a gasoline truck.

This message started in Romania in 1995. It cannot die. If it does, everyone who has been touched by it will experience tragedy. You may ignore it, but it will not ignore you.

You start to write Tina a jokey reply, but stop. A chill quivers down your body as you think of the lost surfer. And the hunched figure in the window. And your own unusually quiet house. You remember how serious Tina seemed about the message.

Still, you can't get yourself to forward it to 13 of your friends. You don't want to inflict it on them. You wonder what makes people write these messages. Are they trying to spread fear? Or did it start with some curse that goes back centuries and has now leaped to the Internet?

You try to forget about it and make yourself do some homework for a little while. But you keep thinking about Eve and how much she wanted you to stay downstairs. You shut down the computer. But by the time you get back down to the living room, Eve has been put to bed. Candace is reading a book.

You say good night to her and climb the steps back to your room. Once you are in bed, you're restless. A sense of foreboding hangs over you. You tell yourself it's just the time of year. But the unearthly yowls of those creepy coyotes reverberate in your ears. And you can't help but wonder if once again tonight, in your dreams, a consuming fire will rise up all around you.

3
THE MANDRAKE HOUSE

You awake to another beautiful late October day. Pulling apart your curtains, you see that while the sun is shining, something new has appeared. Long, delicately ribbed clouds scurry high in the sky. They seem distant, like mere decoration to an otherwise serene day. But you know they're forerunners of a storm.

Just as you're finishing breakfast, a knock comes at the front door. It's Randy. "Come on!" he says. "And bring your bike."

"How come?" you ask.

"I'll tell you in a minute. Tina's waiting for us."

You get your bike from the garage and head out. Tina lives one block over, and you and Randy usually meet up with her to walk to school. She's waiting on the corner for you, flipping her skateboard up into her hand.

"What's going on?" she says as soon as you arrive.

Randy dives right in. "I talked to my mom about that house we saw last night. You know, the one that belonged to Tibias Mandrake. I think we need to pay another visit."

"Why's that?" you ask.

"We were right," Randy explains. "No one's supposed to be in the house. She thought it was very weird that a light was on. And if you really did see someone..."

You recall the image of the hunched person in the window.

"Yeah, I'm sure someone was there."

"We have to go check it out then," Randy announces.

"Did they ever find that lost surfer?" you ask.

Tina shakes her head. "My dad said no one was found out there. But no one's been reported missing, either. The Coast Guard and police are still on watch."

"Uh," you mention, hating to state the obvious, "shouldn't we just call the police about the house, too?"

Tina gives you a little punch in the shoulder with a leather-wrapped fist. She's been designing new protective gear for riding her skateboard. Her hand is swathed in scrap leather. The strips entwine with a series of tight black laces in a long cuff that covers her wrist. She looks like some kind of futuristic warrior who rides a skateboard instead of a horse.

"Sure, we'll call the police if we find out something is up," she says. "But the Digital Detectives found the evidence, so we get first crack at an investigation."

You shrug. "I'm game. But it's a pretty weird place. Let's go in the daylight."

"Exactly," Randy concurs. "That's why I told you to bring your bike. We're going right after school today."

Tina flexes her fingers, each of which has been carefully wrapped with ragged suede strips. "We'll give that house a complete and thorough examination."

You regard her. Not only are her hands all wrapped up, she's got protective padding on her elbows and knees, too. She wears them out quickly, so she's constantly scavenging for materials to make new ones. Lately she's been on a hunt for a really good helmet. It's all part of the persona she's creating for herself for skateboard competitions: Menace 2U.

"Tina," you say, only half-serious, "was there was ever a

time in your life when you were just a sweet little girl in a dress with a big bow in the back?"

Randy laughs. "Oh yeah, I remember Tina in second grade. Nothing but freckles on her face, and a bunny-white dress just like you said."

Tina makes a fist. "Yeah, how do you think I ended up like this, anyway?"

Randy gets on his bike. "It'll be fun to check out the Mandrake house. Besides, we'll help my mom. Now let's go, or we'll be late for school."

✳ ✳ ✳

You, Randy, and Tina meet Jack at lunch to fill him in on the plan.

"Here's the deal," Randy explains. "Tibias Mandrake died seven years ago. He left instructions in his will that said his nearest relative should inherit the house and the eighty acres of land that go with it. But he forgot to say who that relative was. Maybe he didn't even know himself. My mom says he turned into kind of a hermit in his later years."

As a real estate agent, Randy's mom is a pretty reliable source for information like this. "Anyway, after a few years, the state decided the house was becoming a hazard. It said that if no heir was found within two years, the property would be auctioned off to the highest bidder. The two years is about to expire—in six days, this coming Wednesday. No heir has come forward."

"So it goes on the block," Jack says. "Where's the problem?"

"The thing is," Randy responds, "my mom and the historic society think it should be preserved as a landmark.

Mandrake made some big discovery early in his career. And the house itself is really unusual. If it's made into a landmark, we can go visit it any time. But meanwhile, there are all these people who want to get their hands on the land."

"That's prime oceanfront real estate," Tina notes.

"Exactly. The last undeveloped land for miles along the coast. Major bucks to be made from it. Most of the people who want to buy it would just tear down the house, boom, like that. Only a select few people would even have access to the area."

"So save it for the coyotes?" Jack says.

"That's right, Jack, keep it wild," Tina answers. "We can all share it."

"Anyway, my mom is really into this," Randy goes on. "She thought the light was suspicious. I say we should check it out."

Jack clears his throat. "This we—I don't mind looking into it, but all four of us don't need—"

"You'll stay at the control center, of course," Tina assures him. "The three of us will investigate the house after school."

"All right," Jack consents. "You've still got the Jack Pack, with all your tools, right?"

It's sitting right beside Randy. He pats it. Inside the pack are the devices Jack invented for use in investigations. They include the JackScan, a handheld scanner that can record patterns like tire tracks, footprints, writing, blood spatters, and even fingerprints, if you dust for them first. There's also a digital camera, a magnifying glass, binoculars, and flashlight.

Jack's crowning achievement is the MicroJack. This is like a souped-up, jet-fueled handheld computer that allows you to organize all of your evidence. It's like a portable crime lab. Not only does it let you collect and compare all of your clues, it's got a wireless connection to the Internet and to voice and e-mail.

"Stay in touch while you're out there," Jack instructs. "I'll keep you covered electronically, the best I can."

"Thanks," Randy says.

The bell rings. Randy turns to you and Tina. "Okay, meet at the bike rack as soon as school is out. Then we head on down to the bluff."

* * *

You're glad to see that the sun is still pretty far up the horizon, as you pedal toward the ocean after school. You would prefer not to get caught out on the bluff after dark.

About a mile out of town, you come to the turnoff. Tina is on her bicycle now. You stopped at her house for her bike, and at Randy's so he could pick up Joe. The cocker spaniel snuggles into a basket on the back of Randy's bike and rides along happily, his ears flopping in the wind.

You turn off onto a small, rutted side road that snakes through coastal brush and woods toward the bluff. The whole area is kind of wild. You don't know it very well, because people tend to stay away from it. Being the last part of the coast that hasn't been built up, it's become a refuge for the hermits and eccentrics of old-time Crescent Bay.

You pass by an old farmhouse, whose clapboards give you a cozy, comfortable feeling. A little farther along, you go by a house with a big aluminum shed beside it. After this, the road narrows and turns to dirt. Small paths split off here and there, disappearing into the bush. At one time the road may have been nice and smooth, but now it's full of rivulets and ruts. Vegetation crowds the road. You ride along it carefully until the Mandrake house comes into view.

You leave your bikes at the iron gate in front. The gate is still closed, but the lock on its chain has been broken. Tina unwraps the chain and opens the gate. A gravel drive leads to the front porch. It's quiet as before.

"Hey," you remember, "the front door is locked. How are we going to get in?"

"We'll find a way," Randy says.

He tries the door first. Still locked. He pounds with the knocker a few times. No answer.

You go around the right side of the house. You test the ground floor windows. Locked.

"Wow, look at this," Tina calls from the back of the house. You run over to join her. "This place could use a little support." She points to the ground. Your eyes widen.

The bluff has eroded underneath one corner of the house. It's hanging in thin air, and beginning to sag.

Then you notice that there's a smaller, square building hidden in some trees about thirty yards from the main house. You go to check it out. It looks like some kind of garage or small barn. But the door is locked, and the only window is high in the gable of the roof.

"Bingo!" You hear Randy exclaim. When you return to the main house, you find him in a little recess in the wall, outside of what you would guess is the kitchen.

"A dog door," Randy announces. "All one of us has to do is wriggle through and go open the front door. I'm too big to fit, but…"

Tina gives you a little push in the back.

"Why me?" you demand.

"Because Joe doesn't know how to unlock the door," Tina answers.

You hold out a fist to do a draw. Tina bounces her fist up and down three times with you. She shows *paper*. You show *rock*.

"Good luck," she says.

You take a deep breath and poke your hands through the flap of the dog door. Stale, rank air rushes into your face. Holding your breath, you put your head in. You have to wriggle your shoulders to get them through the opening. Then you walk forward on your hands until the rest of your body follows. Joe comes in right after you.

Finally, you have to let out your breath. As you inhale, a mixture of dust, rot, animal scent, and other odors too gross to contemplate greet your nose. You get to your feet and open your eyes. The first thing you see is...

 Find out on the
Digital Detectives web site:

http://www.ddmysteries.com
and enter the key phrase **MANSION**

When you've finished this investigation,
the web site will give you a page number
to return to.

You close the door of the Mandrake house behind you. "Pretty weird place, huh?" you comment to Randy and Tina.

"Pretty cool stuff," Tina comments. As you walk down the driveway to leave, she stops and looks back. "I wonder..." she goes on.

"Me too," Randy chimes in.

"What?" you ask, afraid they're going to want to go back inside.

"Did we look in all the rooms that we should have?" Tina says. "I have a feeling we might have missed something."

You sigh. "Don't tell me you want to go back in, too."

Randy gives an apologetic shrug. "I just have a feeling there's more in there. There were a lot of rooms."

Tina tugs on your sleeve. "Come on. It's still light out. Let's go back inside. This time, I'll go through the dog door."

"Just watch out for animals," you warn. You sigh again and turn back to the Mandrake house.

Return to the Digital Detectives web site to do some more investigation:

http://www.ddmysteries.com

and enter the key phrase **LEFTMANSION**

When you've finished this investigation, the web site will give you a page number to return to.

You stand quivering in the closet where you've taken refuge. Somewhere you hear a yelp from Joe, and suddenly you realize you should have brought him in here with you, too. Then again, the coyote was between you and him. Maybe you couldn't have reached him even if you tried.

You pray Joe is able to escape the animal. If he can't, you don't know how you'll face Randy. You'll never forgive yourself.

You keep listening at the door. All you can hear is your own gasping breath. It's pitch black inside the closet. The darkness only makes your heart pound harder. In a moment of panic, you want to open the door. But then an image of the coyote's bared teeth comes back. You stay put.

Then, a couple of minutes later, the door bursts open. You shrink back onto the floor of the closet, covering your face.

"It's you!" Tina shrieks.

Your fingers slip down over your face. "It's you," you moan with relief. "Is the coyote gone?"

"Yes," Randy says from behind her. "Tina came in after you when we heard Joe's barks. She chased the coyote out the dog door."

Blood rushes to your face. Your hands go back over your face. You've never been this embarrassed before. "Sorry," you mumble. "Is Joe—"

"He's fine," Randy says, offering a hand to pull you to your feet. "Don't worry about it. That coyote was pretty nasty."

Tina gives you a sympathetic smile as well. "Let's get to work."

You smile back weakly. You wish you'd been as brave as her, but there's no time to feel sorry for yourself. You've got an investigation to do.

Return to your investigation
on the Digital Detectives web site:

http://www.ddmysteries.com
and enter the key phrase COYOTES

When you've finished this investigation, the web site will give you a page number to return to.

4
THE SHADOWS

"The question isn't *if* something is going on at the old Mandrake house," Randy declares. "The question is *how much!*"

The Digital Detectives have gathered in Randy's living room. It's almost dinner time. Dusk is falling outside.

"One thing is easy to see," you respond. "Someone is living there. Or has been living there. It looks like they might have left in a hurry."

"Someone who needs help," Randy agrees.

"If we assume that's who wrote HELP on the window," Jack puts in. "What if it was some random person three years ago?"

"No, it was too fresh," you assert. "But you're right, we shouldn't make conclusions until we can do more investigation."

"Yeah, there could be more than one person," Tina agrees, thrusting a leg out to rest it on the coffee table. All of the decor in the room matches, from the flower print sofa to the handcrafted vases. The only thing that clashes is Tina. She's still in her thrashing gear, which includes a kneepad made from gauze and foam and a patch of neoprene cut from an old wetsuit.

"Did you see the video titles upstairs?" she continues. "They were a weird mix of opera and science fiction. Same

31

with the food cartons. There was frozen pizza, but there was also gourmet stuff. Plus those comic books.

"Whoever they are, they're pretty creepy. All those weird symbols—and the bones—and the ashes. What do you think is going on?" you wonder.

"I guess some of that stuff could have been left over from Tibias Mandrake," Jack says. "He was a total eccentric."

"We should try to find out more about him," you suggest. "We should interview people in that farmhouse on the way out. And maybe you can ask people about him on your web site, Randy."

"Good idea," Randy agrees. He runs a site, with Jack's help, that serves as a kind of unofficial newspaper for the school and neighborhood. It's called WhatISay.net.

"And what about the animals?" you add. "They acted as if they owned the place."

Randy laughs. "Poor Joe isn't used to having to share his space with creatures from the wild. But to them, the house is just part of their habitat now."

"That place is returning to the wild, all right," Tina says. "I get the feeling some kind of strange rituals are taking there, too. It'd be cool to go out some night and see what they are."

"*Cool?*" you blurt.

Jack frowns. "Your ideas of cool have gotten pretty weird lately, Tina. What is the deal with that spam you sent us?"

"Spam? Someone warns you about a virus, that's not spam," Tina retorts. "It's a fair warning. I happen to know what came down for some kids who didn't pass it on."

"Anybody can make up stories for the Internet," Jack scoffs.

Tina flinches, looking hurt that Jack won't take the e-mail seriously. "These are kids *here*, Jack. In Crescent Bay. This girl named Jane had every single thing in her locker stolen. Another girl got a bad case of poison oak. Please forward the message. As a favor to me."

Jack rolls his eyes. "We're detectives. Detectives don't believe in superstition."

Tina's green eyes flash. She jabs a leather-wrapped finger at him. "You don't believe in *anything* that can't be reduced to bits and bytes. What if there are powers in the world that can't be digitized?"

Jack holds up his hands in surrender. "Sorry. But I deleted it already. I'll just have to take what's coming to me."

Tina shifts her glare to you and Randy. "What about you? Have you forwarded it yet?"

"Uh, I'm still getting my list together," you offer lamely.

Randy is saved from answering by the sound of the front door opening. It's his mother, Diane Rivers. She's dressed for work, an elegant scarf wrapped across her shoulders. Her dark hair is loose and a little bit windblown. Her eyes have friendly wrinkles around them.

"Hello, everyone," she says.

After you all say hello, Randy asks a question. "Hey mom, we have some stuff we should tell you about that house Mr. Mandrake used to live in."

Diane takes off her scarf and sits down. "Yes, let's have a firsthand report. I've been hearing about this all afternoon."

"What?" all four of you ask at once.

"You must have already told someone, haven't you?" she says. "Word has been circulating like wildfire in real estate circles. It's a small world, you know, so news gets around fast."

"But," you sputter, "we haven't told anyone about it."

"Not one person," Randy confirms. "What have you heard?"

"That there appears to be some mighty odd things going on in that house," Diane answers. "Black magic. Animal sacrifice. That sort of thing."

"Where did these stories come from?" Jack asks. "If we knew who started them, that might give us a lead."

"I'll try to find out," Diane says. "But you know, there have been stories going around about Tibias Mandrake for a long time. He was a colorful figure."

Randy nods. "I remember some of the older kids talking about knocking on his door as a Halloween dare."

She bites her lip. "But animal sacrifices, rituals—this isn't good for the historical society. We have a lot of support for turning the house into a historic landmark, but this might scare people away."

"Well," Randy says, "we didn't see any animal sacrifices, but it did look like someone has been living there."

Diane frowns. "That might be the worst thing of all. Do you have any idea who it is?"

"There might be more than one person," you say.

Diane looks perplexed. "I wonder what's going on. There are plenty of people who'd like to see us fail at getting landmark status for the house. People who have other plans for it, if it goes up for auction."

"What kind of other plans?" Randy asks.

"A golf course," his mom answers. "Subdivisions. A private estate. You can see everyone who's interested down at the county courthouse tonight. A meeting is scheduled to tell people about the property and how the auction will work, if they have one."

"You mean if no heir to Mandrake is found in the next three days?" Jack puts in.

"It seems unlikely one will be found now, if they haven't been for seven years," Diane points out. "I'm hoping we can get the property declared a landmark before the auction ever takes place."

"We'll come," Tina says. She taps her watch. "But right now, I've got to go fix dinner for my dad. Should we meet back here afterward?"

"You're welcome to," Diane replies. "You can all ride down with me."

✳ ✳ ✳

The meeting about the Mandrake house takes place in a room on the second floor of the courthouse. A state official named Mr. Rundell stands before a room full of people, mostly well-dressed adults sitting in folding chairs. He announces that in view of the fact that no heir to Tibias Mandrake has been found, preparations are under way to put the property up for auction next week.

He explains the rules of the auction. Bids for the house should be delivered in a sealed envelope by noon on Wednesday, November 1. The bids will be opened at five o'clock that day and the winner will be announced.

After giving some more details, Mr. Rundell asks for questions. A woman with light brown hair rises to speak, ignoring the other raised hands, as if she owns the floor.

"That's Betsy Akers," Diane whispers. "She's an agent. Driven to succeed, ever since her divorce. She represents some secret client."

You check her out. She wears a beige business suit, pearls, and very fashionable glasses. Very serious looking, you decide.

"In light of rumors that have come up today," Betsy Akers demands, "shouldn't the police investigate the house before we are asked to put up money in our bids?"

"What rumors are those?" asks Mr. Rundell.

"That the house is being used for some sort of appalling rituals. Everyone knows about them," Betsy says with disdain. "Unless it's just a story some kids made up," she adds with a glance in your direction.

You want to jump up and defend yourself, but you just grip your seat.

Instead, a man in a polo shirt and leather jacket stands to answer her. He has short blond hair, pink skin, and a perfectly straight nose. "Come now, Betsy," he says in a snooty voice. "You're not afraid of ghosts, are you? If your client has such a weak stomach, perhaps the property is not for him. Whomever he or she is."

"Bill Cabot," Diane whispers. "A developer. Went to Princeton. Wants to build a golf course on the property."

Betsy's eyes remain fixed on Rundell like a hawk. "Well?" she demands, as if Bill Cabot never spoke.

"I'll ask the police to investigate first thing in the morning," Mr. Rundell promises.

Diane stands up to have her say. "I'm glad to hear the police will be checking into the house. Tibias Mandrake was a unique figure in Crescent Bay. The house is a historic site. I understand a VCR and some videos were found upstairs. Someone may be living there illegally."

"Ridiculous," Bill Cabot declares. "I'm sure the house has

no electricity."

"Ask my son about that," Diane replies.

She looks at Randy. His expression says it all: *Don't do this to me, Mom!* But he doesn't have any choice. He stands up and lists a few of things you found that indicate the place was inhabited. A few concerned gasps go through the audience when he mentions finding the word HELP scrawled in the dust. Randy does pretty well, considering he's got all these serious grown-ups staring at him.

"That's all very interesting, Diane," Bill Cabot says with a smirk. "But let's wait until some real detectives get a look at the place."

Randy's face flushes red as he sits down. You give him a pat on the shoulder and whisper, "We'll show him."

"Are there any other questions?" Mr. Rundell asks.

"I assume there will be a written report on the condition of the house," Betsy Akers states.

"We'll do our best," Rundell promises. "Now, I have printed information up here in front if you have any more questions. This meeting is concluded."

Rundell ducks out of the room before he can get nailed by another question. The room buzzes. Those who haven't heard the rumors about the house want to know all about them. You overhear all kinds of wild things being described. Some of what you hear matches up with what you discovered at the house, but most is major fantasy.

A knot of people crowd around Randy and Diane, wanting to know what he found. Randy gives only a bare minimum of information.

Tina and Jack slip out of the knot in order to avoid answering questions. You're doing the same, when you spot a man sitting in the back of the room. You notice him because he remains motionless amidst the commotion. His hair is dark, streaked with silver, and combed back. His silver-black mustache is neatly clipped. He wears a fancy suit and sleek leather shoes.

Your eyes fall to a large ring on his finger. It's stamped with the same crest you saw above Mandrake's fireplace.

You touch Diane's elbow and point to the man. "Mrs. Rivers, do you know who he is?"

Diane peers at him. "No. He looks familiar, but I can't place him."

You make your way over to Tina and Jack. They're in a corner, talking to two other kids who came to the meeting. The kids are a few grades ahead of you. They're dressed mostly in black. As you join the group, the girl is talking to Jack.

"I know you," she says, regarding him from hooded eyes rimmed with black makeup. Her eyebrows are thin slashes. "You're the genius with computers. You have some kind of nickname, like a space station."

"Satellite Jack," Tina tells her. She notices you, and introduces the pair. The boy's name is Mordar. The girl's name is Sorrow.

Before you can ask if those are their real names, Mordar looks you up and down. "What's your name?" he asks.

You tell him. He tilts his chin up and repeats your name. The way he rolls it around on his tongue makes you feel like you've just given up some very personal information.

Then it occurs to you where you've seen his name before. "You started that chain letter," you declare. "The one about how bad things will happen if you don't forward it."

His lips draw back from his teeth. "I hope you followed the instructions."

"I did what I always do with messages that say 'do not delete'," Jack announces proudly. "Killed it."

Sorrow says, "You shouldn't tempt fate like that. The Internet is a powerful force."

"Maybe *the force* is with *me*," Jack jokes.

Sorrow gazes at him for a moment. Her hair is a peculiar color of black. It has no reflection, and seems only to absorb light. Her blue eyes gleam unnaturally from under the hair and eye shadow. "Have you ever contacted a dead person through the Net?"

Jack wrinkles his brow. "Do they have modems in heaven?"

"You might be surprised, Mr. Science," Mordar replies. "I'll send you some URLs. See for yourself."

Sorrow gives Jack a dismissive wave. "Your technology is so primitive. It can't detect shadows. We've been in touch with Tibias Mandrake using nothing but a…well, I guess that's our secret."

Your jaw drops open in the exact same way that Tina and Jack's do. "Tibias Mandrake?" Tina gasps. "How did you contact him? Is he alive?"

"Of course not," Mordar replies with disdain. "And we didn't contact him. He contacted us."

A smile spreads across Sorrow's face as she takes in your stunned expressions. She wiggles her black-painted fingernails at you and says, "So long."

As the pair leaves, you glance over at Jack. He stares after them with a bemused smile of his own. "I think those two need defragmenting," he comments.

5

THE RUMOR MILL

Some nameless anxiety clouds your mind the next day. You don't know why, but you feel out of sorts. The morning drags on until finally the lunch bell rings and you join the other three Digital Detectives at a table in the lunchroom. They look as gloomy as you feel.

"What's going on?" you ask. "Or is it just me?"

"No, it's not just you," Randy replies glumly. "I just talked to my mom. The police checked out the Mandrake house this morning. They found nothing."

Your eyes widen. "The VCR? The tapes? The food—"

"Nada," Randy confirms. "Someone must have cleared all that stuff out last night. We look like chumps. Everyone's going to be laughing at us."

"This only confirms that something really is going on," Tina states. "Obviously whoever was there is afraid of getting caught."

"You're right," Jack agrees. "But we don't know if a major crime is involved. Maybe it was just some hobo who needed a place to live."

"A hobo with a VCR?" Tina says. "Where'd the power come from, anyway?"

"Probably a portable generator," Jack answers.

"Whatever, I want to get to the bottom of it," Randy says. "My mom agrees there's something weird going on. At least *she* believes us. I don't know if anyone else does. The police just laughed when she asked about the HELP message and said anybody could have written it. As if we might have written it just to, I don't know, get publicity."

Jack sighs deeply and adjusts the frames of his glasses on his face. "You're right," he says thoughtfully. He finally seems to be taking the matter seriously. "Our reputation is at stake now. Whether there's a crime or not, we need to figure out what's going on out there in order to clear our name."

"Yes," you agree, as the full meaning of the police report dawns on you. "Another thing I'd like to know is, how did those rumors get started? About the animal sacrifices and all."

"There have been rumors about Tibias since forever," Jack points out.

"But the worst of them started on the very day of our investigation," Randy counters.

"Someone must have seen us out there," Tina surmises. "Whoever is doing what they're doing out there is crafty. By spreading the rumors, they discredited our investigation before we even really started."

"It's as if they're one step ahead of us," you say.

Tina shakes her head. "Creepy. Well, there's only one thing we can do. More investigation. Go back to the house."

"We'll get a chance to do that tomorrow," Randy says. "My mom is going to give a tour of the house for the Landmark Commission and anyone else who wants to see it. She hopes to convince people to make it into a historic landmark. I think we should go on the tour and see what we can see."

"I'm there," you say.

"I guess I should see this place, too," Jack decides. "I'll bring my latest investigation tools."

"Good. Now what else can we do?" Tina drums her fingers on the table. "Let's interview the neighbors in the area, find out what they've seen."

"Yes," Randy agrees. "We can do that when we go out for the tour."

"Let's find out more about the auction, too," you add. "Maybe that Mr. Rundell will talk to us at the courthouse."

"Okay, we can go down there after school," Randy says.

"I'll be busy practicing on the half-pipe," Tina says. "Gotta keep working on my frontside 50-50s. But call me tonight. This whole thing is bizarre."

Well, that clinches it. The Digital Detectives are on the case. You know that if Tina declares something bizarre, she won't stop until she finds out more.

You notice she's wearing nail polish. It's a murky, flat color that makes you squirm, though it's hard to put your finger on why.

"What's that color on your nails?" you ask.

"Coffin," Tina says, spreading her fingers.

Jack can't resist. "*Coffin*? That's a *color*?"

Tina ignores him. "Sorrow gave it to me. I might use it for my skateboard outfit. The Shadows have given me a bunch of good ideas for that."

"The Shadows?" Randy repeats.

"That's what they call themselves. There's about seven of them. Mordar and Sorrow are the leaders."

"Those aren't their real names." You state this as a fact, not a question.

"Who's to say?" Tina replies. "Which one of my names is real—Menace, or Tina? Which describes me best?"

Jack scratches his temple as if pondering something. "So I guess that means that if they get a threatening chain letter, bad stuff won't happen to them personally. Just to the character with the funny name."

"Fine, Jack," Tina snaps. "Don't believe it. But don't make fun of other people's beliefs, okay?"

Tina's eyes stray to a table behind you. You turn around to look. Mordar and Sorrow are at the table with some other kids dressed like them.

"So you're friends with them, Tina?" you ask.

She shrugs. "Sort of. Sorrow started talking to me because she liked my elbow pads."

"So, what's this about them hearing the ghost of Tibias Mandrake?" you go on. "How do they know about him?"

"I'm not sure," Tina answers. "I'll try to find out. Maybe I'll tell them about the tour. But you have to be careful. They can turn on you. I've seen them do it to other people."

"Like fish under a hot sun," Jack agrees. He regards their table. The Shadows are standing up and getting ready to leave. "Give them another message, too." He waits, but Tina won't bite. "Tell them that Halloween isn't until Tuesday."

Tina gets up without a word. Jack's grin fades as she walks off without looking back. "Miss Grumpy," he remarks.

"Stop ragging on Tina, Jack," Randy advises. "We've got a case to solve."

It's amazing how quickly Jack's face can go from smug and smart to peevish and disappointed. On the rare occasion when he is wrong, Jack isn't happy to admit it.

As you stand up to leave, you glance at the table where the Shadows were sitting. Some markings have been left on it. You take the digital camera out of your pack, and go over to have a look.

* * *

You find Mr. Rundell sitting at his desk. His jacket hangs from the back of his chair, and he's wearing suspenders and a striped shirt.

You give a little knock at his open door. "Excuse me?"

He swivels in his chair and gives you a suspicious glare.

"Your secretary was gone, so..."

"What can I do for you?"

"We'd like to ask you about Tibias Mandrake's house."

His eyes flick to Randy. "You're Diane Rivers' son, aren't you? Sure, sit down. You heard about the police report?"

"Yes," Randy answers. He quickly introduces you and Jack. The three of you perch on chairs in front of Rundell's desk.

"So, I don't think there's any problems out there," Rundell says. "That's what the police tell me."

"We really did see what I said we did," Randy replies. "Not the really weird stuff, but evidence that.. someone was living here."

Rundell just grunts. Seeing that you're getting nowhere, you change the subject. "Can you tell us more about the auction?" you ask.

"It's not all that complicated," Rundell replies. "You decide how much you're willing to pay for it. Write your bid down and seal it in an envelope. We open the envelopes Wednesday afternoon. Highest bid wins, so long as the financing arrangements check out." He stretches his arms behind his head, leans back, and adds, "Why, are you planning to submit a bid?"

Randy laughs, which you realize is exactly the right response. You don't want Rundell to realize how serious about investigating you are. "No, we're just trying to figure out who would have an interest in meddling with the house."

"Are you working for your mom?" Rundell asks bluntly.

Randy shrugs. "I want to help her, of course. Does she have to bid for the house like everyone else?"

Rundell yawns. He doesn't bother to cover his mouth; his hands stay locked behind his head. "Depends. If she can persuade the Landmark Commission that the house has historic value, they might remove the land from development. She might succeed, too. She's got a lot of people on her side. Somehow she's managed to convince them that lunatic's place is worth preserving."

"What's the Landmark Commission?" you ask.

"State body that oversees historic sites. Now, have I answered all your questions?"

"What if something were to happen that made people nervous about the house?" Randy queries. "What if someone's trying to scare people away from it?"

Rundell gives an indulgent smile. "It's scary enough already, don't you think?" He checks his watch. "Now, if you'll excuse me, I've got some real work to do," he says, shooing you out of his office. You want to snap his suspenders.

The three of you walk silently down the stairs. You feel bummed by how Rundell treated you. Could it be that no one takes you seriously any more?

You reach the bike rack outside the courthouse before Randy breaks the silence. "What a doily."

You and Jack just nod in agreement. As you bend down to unlock your bike, you notice some black-clad figures across the street. It's Sorrow and Mordar, in front of an ice cream store. They're bent over a bicycle, which is locked to a parking sign. You gaze idly at them for a minute, until Mordar happens to glance up and meet your eyes. He makes no acknowledgment, but says something to Sorrow. They straighten up and walk briskly away, leaving the bike behind.

"You guys want an ice cream cone?" you ask Randy and Jack.

"Definitely," Jack says. "I need something to get the bad taste out of my mouth."

You walk your bikes across the street. As you approach the store, a kid in your class comes out. His name is Danny. He pops the tail end of a cone into his mouth, then unlocks the bike at the parking sign and jumps on it. The front wheel wobbles wildly as he begins to ride toward you.

"Danny, stop!" you cry.

You see Danny's hands work the brakes. But instead of stopping, he falls over, right on the sidewalk, nearly crashing into a woman carrying groceries. The woman gives him a dirty look and walks away. You run up.

"Danny, you all right? What happened?"

"Yeah, I'm okay," Danny says, dusting himself off. He inspects a scrape on his elbow, then kicks his tire. "Man, stupid bike!"

"What's wrong with it?" Randy asks.

"Aw, nothing," Danny admits. His shoulders sag. "I guess I should've been more careful. I was warned something like this might happen."

"What do you mean?" you probe.

"I got this stupid e-mail a few days ago, a chain letter," Danny says. "It said if I didn't send it to thirteen people—"

"We know all about it," you interrupt. "Do you know the Shadows—Sorrow and Mordar?"

Danny scrunches up his face. "I'm not sure. What do they have to do with it?"

"Never mind," you respond. "Just keep that e-mail on your computer as evidence, okay?"

"Sure," he says, then looks after you and Randy and Jack, mystified, as you get on your bikes and ride away.

It occurs to you to look down and check the tires and brakes on your own bike. But they're all right.

After all, you realize, the four days since you got *your* chain e-mail aren't up yet.

6
THE TOUR

You head over to Randy's house around noon the next day, Saturday. Puffy clouds have filled the sky. The wind is blowing the coming storm your way. It's supposed to arrive tomorrow.

Tina is already there, in Randy's driveway. She's wearing a new tint of nail polish, but you're afraid to ask what it is. Probably Puke or Death, you figure.

Jack shows up a few minutes later. You watch him approach on his BMX bike and can't help but laugh a little. He wobbles around on the high seat and high handlebars. The little frame can barely balance him. Something happened to his parents on Jack's last birthday. They had some kind of brain burp and gave him the bike as a present. What were they thinking?

The four of you set off for the Mandrake house. Cars are parked on the lawn at the mansion. People mill around, testing the front door, which is still locked.

A number of the people who came to the auction meeting are there. Bill Cabot is carrying a golf club and practicing his swing on the lawn. A blond kid whose hair sticks straight up in a buzz cut is with him. Randy tells you that he's Cabot's son, Trip, who goes to a private school. He's got an upturned nose, shiny skin, and cold blue eyes. He surveys the property as if he owns the place.

Betsy Akers is there, too, looking annoyed as the sea breeze messes up her hair. You also notice Sorrow and Mordar lurking by the chimney. And the mysterious man with the Mandrake crest on his ring is leaning against a wall. Plus, there are several other people who you guess must be members of the Landmark Commission and the Crescent Bay Historical Society.

Diane mounts the steps to the main house and calls for attention. "Everyone, we're about ready to start the tour. I'll tell you a little bit about the house, then we can begin."

The crowd gathers around the steps and Diane begins her introduction. "Tibias Mandrake was a true original. In his younger days, he was celebrated for a major discovery in the field of paleontology. We don't know why he chose Crescent Bay, but this is where he spent his later years pursuing some very interesting and esoteric research. The house itself was designed according to his theories about how the human brain evolved."

Trip Cabot lets out a long, bored sigh and mutters, "Must be what turned him crazy in the end."

"One of the things that makes him so interesting," Diane goes on, "is that he became rather reclusive toward the end of his life. We don't know the exact nature of his later research, but the rumor is it involved the re-animation of prehistoric—"

Betsy Akers interrupts. "I don't believe he published much after his original discovery, did he Diane?"

"Perhaps not…" Diane answers slowly, looking at some of the other members of the Historical Society. They shake their heads.

"So really, this is not a valid aspect of his legacy," Betsy says.

"My understanding is that he was not respected in the local scientific community, to put it mildly. Perhaps we should get to what we all came here for—the house itself."

Diane appears flustered. "Um, well, that's fine..." She nods sharply. "Yes, let's go inside," she says, trying to recover herself. "I'll be seeing it for the first time myself since Mr. Mandrake died, so it should be fascinating."

trying to recover herself. "I'll be seeing the inside for the first time myself since Mr. Mandrake died, so it should be a fascinating."

Bill Cabot raises his golf club and proclaims, "To the house!"

Diane turns to the door and fumbles for a set of keys in her purse. She tries several, but none of them seem to fit. Bill marches up and says, "Allow me."

After a few minutes of effort, he announces, "Diane, I don't believe you've got the right key!"

Diane's face turns red. "But that's the set Mr. Rundell gave me."

Everyone stares at her. It's a very embarrassing situation for Randy's mother. Her mouth opens and closes as she tries to think of what to say.

Suddenly, you have an idea. "I'll get the door open!" you announce. "Everyone wait here."

You race around to the side of the house and wriggle in through the dog door. You dash up the hallway and fling open the front door with a grand gesture.

People clap. "Thank you," Diane Rivers exhales.

Everyone has something to say to you as they file in. Most of them are nice, except for Bill Cabot. "You're quite the little housebreaker, aren't you?" he remarks, regarding you with narrowed eyes.

You wait until everyone has gone into the house. Randy stays with his mom as the crowd moves into the living room, but Jack and Tina hang back with you in the entry hall.

"We're missing the tour," Jack says.

"Been here. Done that," Tina replies.

"We'll give you our own tour," you agree. "You've got to see the library."

Jack gasps when you enter the two-story room. "Man, look at all these dead trees!"

"No, Jack," Tina corrects him. "Check out that totally radical tapestry. I'll bet it's from the Middle Ages. Those people knew how to make your skin crawl."

Jack studies it. "You got that right," he comments. He shudders.

Tina is listening at the door. "It sounds like the tour has moved on," she says. "Come on and check out the living room."

You head back into the living room. But you stop dead in your tracks when you come through the door. Sorrow and Mordar are in front of the fireplace. Kissing.

"Please!" Jack exclaims. "Have some respect for the dead!"

Jack's probably a lot more bothered by the kissing than by the fact it's in a dead person's house. But the two Shadows part. A knowing smile slices across Sorrow's face. "Maybe he's dead to *you*."

You decide it's time to be bold. "So what's this about you talking to Tibias?"

Mordar and Sorrow look at each other. You notice that their nostrils are lined with a fine edge of black makeup. It's the first time you've ever seen nostril shadow. The liner is smudged from the smooching.

"He was a very gentle man," Mordar says. "But he was driven by an obsession to find out about life. What is its driving force?"

Sorrow spreads her arms to the room and heaves a sigh of awe. "He was on the verge of finding it here. Re-animation. The secret of life."

"And death," Mordar adds. "He's going to reveal it to us."

Jack gives a snort. "And is he the one who tells you which people's bikes to sabotage, because they supposedly have a curse on them?"

"That does not compute," Mordar answers calmly.

"We saw you outside the ice cream store," you say. "You know we did."

Mordar pretends to think. "Oh yeah. We saw this kid's bike was messed up. We were just fixing it for him."

Jack's brain is working quickly. "How'd you know it was a boy?"

"I could tell," Mordar replies loftily. He links his arm through Sorrow's. "Now if you don't mind, we'll continue our tour of the estate."

Sorrow eyes Tina, who glances away. Sorrow giggles with Mordar as they stroll out of the room. "*We* should be giving the tour," she declares.

You plop yourself down on the sofa. A cloud of dust mushrooms up around you. "Well, that cleared that up. They were definitely sabotaging Danny's bike."

Tina frowns. "Come on, it takes more evidence that that. Besides, we need these guys. They might have important information about Tibias and the house."

Jack rolls his eyes. "That's all right, I'll look it up on the

Psychic Freaks Network."

Tina scowls at him. "Jack, you of all people should appreciate someone who's *different*. Who's not normal."

Jack pauses, a finger on his lip. "It's true I'm quite a bit above average. But there's different and then there's different. Those two are a couple of pixels short of a full screen."

You don't want Tina and Jack to start arguing again, so you jump to your feet. "Let's go up and look at that bedroom again," you suggest.

The three of you make your way up the stairs. The bedroom at the top is completely empty, except for the bed frame and a bare mattress.

"The police were right," you say. "Everything is gone."

"It's the only room with no dust. That should have made the police suspicious," Jack says.

Tina is busy inspecting the windows. "They missed this."

She points to the letters in the dust written backwards so that someone outside the window would read H - E - L - P. You stare at them, wondering what kind of terror their author felt in this room.

Then you notice movement outside the window. The room looks over the ocean. A small figure is visible down on the narrow beach. You grab Tina and Jack and point.

"Someone with a surfboard," you observe. You squint harder. He's got long blond hair, and looks pretty tall.

"He must have paddled in," Tina says. "I'll bet it's low tide right now."

The surfer gazes up at the house. He seems to be staring directly at you, almost as if he heard you. You remain motionless. Then, he waves and gives a thumbs-up.

"What's he doing?" Tina wonders.

Jack grabs you. "Come on! He must be signaling to someone in another room!"

You dash out of the room and down the hall. The first door you try is a bathroom. A woman from the Historical Society screams when you burst in. "Sorry!" you say, blushing furiously. You back out quickly.

The next door is shut, too. The room is dark, and at first you think it's empty. Then, you make out two figures near the closed drapes. It's Sorrow and Mordar, kissing again.

"Bleah!" Jack blurts, turning around.

Tina leads you down the hall to the next room. No one's in there, but you hear voices coming from one room down.

Tina approaches it carefully. The door is open. You peek around the corner. You figure this must have been the master bedroom. It's fairly large, and several people are inside it. You pull back and take your digital camera from the JackPack. Meanwhile, Jack fishes around inside it to find his wireless microphone.

You add a periscope attachment to the camera, which allows you to take pictures around the corner. Through the camera's viewfinder, you see that Bill and Betsy are facing each other across the bed. Another realtor, a woman whom you recognize from the meeting, stands near the wardrobe, and the unknown man in the trench coat is seated on a chair.

Jack places the mike under the doorjamb as you snap some pictures. Then, you retreat to the empty room next door. Jack powers up his receiver, and you listen in on the conversation. The first voice you hear is the realtor's: "Nice view, indeed," she says. So what do you think—will the Historical

Society succeed in preserving this place?"

"Please," Bill Cabot scoffs. "A bunch of old ladies drinking tea."

"Diane Rivers is a formidable woman," Betsy counters. "She's lined up all the right people to get landmark status.

The realtor nods. "It's a fascinating house, I must say. Especially with all the rumors of weird rites and spirits,"

Betsy raises her eyebrows. "Are you the one who started those rumors?"

"Heavens no," she protests. "I was only wondering if the house will actually go up for auction. But perhaps you know something that I don't."

"I'll tell you something you don't know," Bill Cabot pronounces heartily. "This time next year, you'll be standing on the ninth green of my golf course."

"That's a charming fantasy, Bill," Betsy answers sweetly.

"You seem strangely confident as well, Betsy, the realtor notes. "Does your mystery client have some secret weapons?"

She gets only silence in reply.

"Well," Bill drawls, "I don't think there's going to be an auction. I think it will be settled before that."

"Quite so," Betsy agrees.

A long silence follows. Bill cracks first. "So, what have you got?"

"You'll find out on Tuesday," Betsy replies. "I'll file the papers by the end of the business day."

"No," Bill says, stricken. "It couldn't be—you don't have an heir to Mandrake, do you?"

"Did I say that?"

"Impossible!" Bill cries.

"See for yourself on Tuesday," she answers.

"Ah, Tuesday. One day before the state's deadline expires," an unfamiliar voice notes. It belongs to the fourth person in the room, the mysterious man in the trench coat. His diction is formal, with a slight Mexican accent. "I'm sure your claim will be examined carefully. Surely it is true that Mandrake was not born out of thin air. Surely he has relatives. One needs only to find them."

"I'm sorry," Betsy says, "did we meet, Mr.—?"

"You know very well who I am," the man replies coolly.

Betsy makes a little "hmph," then you hear her heels clicking toward the door.

"I've got a relative of Mandrake's too," Bill calls after her. "And he'll beat yours! You'll see my papers by Tuesday afternoon as well!"

"Whatever you say, Bill," Betsy purrs as she exits.

You gape at Jack and Tina. "Wow, this changes *everything*."

"No kidding," Jack observes. "If either one of them has an heir to Mandrake on their side, Randy's mom is in big trouble."

"Yes," Tina agrees. "And they're planning to blindside her on Tuesday."

7
THE MACKERS

Sunday starts an hour late. That's because the clocks changed overnight, falling back from Pacific Daylight to Pacific Standard Time. Darkness will come an hour earlier now.

Pulling open your curtains this morning, you see that low gray clouds have moved in. The air is humid and still, waiting for the storm to unleash.

You hurry over to Randy's house. His mother invited all of the Digital Detectives over for brunch. Diane is serving up pancakes, eggs, sausage, bacon, muffins and just about anything else you can think of to eat.

She went to a historical society dinner last night, so she hasn't been filled in yet on what you overheard during the tour yesterday. She furrows her brow as Tina tells her that Bill Cabot said he's found an heir to Mandrake.

"Bill's not one to make idle claims," Diane muses as she sits down with a plate of eggs and sausage. "He's very 'old school'. They usually say less than they know, rather than more. I'm surprised that he let it slip."

"I think that he was goaded by Betsy Akers," you point out. "She sounded so confident she would get the house. I think that she's found an heir, too."

Diane shakes her head. "But we searched the genealogy records up and down. How could they each have found one?"

"We've gone from zero to two heirs in about thirty seconds," Randy muses.

Diane throws up her hands. "And I'm sure that there are more out there, somewhere. We just can't find any of them to be on our side!"

"I don't quite get it," Jack says. "How does finding a relative of Mandrake's give Bill or Betsy the estate?"

"No doubt that they've set up a very nice deal to transfer the property," Diane responds with a sigh. "These relatives probably never knew Tibias and couldn't care less about the house. They just want the money. Oh, this is so sad."

"How come, Mom?" Randy asks.

"Because, the house—well, you saw it. It's one of a kind. It may be weird, it may be creepy, but it's a treasure. Both in terms of science and architecture. It's part of our history. Don't you want to be able to take your kids down there and tell them all about this character, Tibias Mandrake?"

"That'd be fun," Tina agrees.

"Well, if Bill or Betsy or some of those other people have their way, the bulldozers will demolish it without a trace," Diane says. "Only an elite few will have access to that part of the coast."

"What are Betsy's plans for it?" you inquire.

"Betsy is being very secretive," Diane answers. "She says she has a 'very big client.' Betsy always acts like her clients are the Queen of England or something. Which I'm sure the clients enjoy."

"And Mr. Cabot wants to build a golf course," Tina says.

Diane spears a link. "Just what this town needs, another golf course. That man—he doesn't just play golf, he's obsessed by it."

"Sick," Jack mutters.

"But you still have an inside track, don't you?" Randy asks his mom. "Everyone's on your side."

She bends her head for a moment and stares deeply into her coffee. "I don't think so, honey. Not if Bill and Betsy come through on their claims."

"How about Mr. Rundell?" Tina wonders. "He'll make sure any alleged heir checks out, won't he?"

Diane takes a sip of coffee that appears especially bitter. "I think Rundell would be perfectly happy to see the house get plowed under. He's a big believer in so-called, 'progress.'"

You all gaze silently at your plates. The eggs suddenly look cold and congealed.

"What about the other man who was in the master bedroom?" you remember. "He had a Spanish accent of some kind."

Diane looks up. "You must mean Carlos Ramirez. That's all I was able to get out of Rundell—his name. He's from Mexico City originally, and now lives in Los Angeles. What he's doing here, no one knows."

"And then there's that surfer on the beach," Randy recalls. "You said he was waving to someone up in the house?"

"Definitely," you reply. "I think he saw someone, then gave a thumbs-up sign. We were trying to find out who it was when we stumbled on the conversation in the bedroom."

"I couldn't believe how they talked," Tina says. "Those people acted like the house was theirs to fight over. As if the whole reason for the tour didn't exist."

Diane sighs, her eyes downcast. "They've got all the money on their side. I don't know what we've got on ours any more." She looks up at you. "I'm sorry, I don't mean to put my problems on you kids. I guess there's nothing we can do."

"Hold on," Randy says. "The Digital Detectives' reputation is at stake, too."

"Yeah," Jack concurs. "Ever since the police found nothing at the house, people have been laughing at us. I got an e-mail calling us the Figital Defectives."

Tina actually laughs at this. Randy and Jack both glower. "We need to prove that we know what we're doing," Randy declares.

"The more I think about it," you say, "the weirder I think it is that that surfer was on the shore below the house. Maybe he was the same surfer we thought was lost the other day. Maybe he wasn't really lost."

"Let's go to the beach this afternoon," Randy says to you. "See if we can find the guy."

"Jack and I can go back to the bluff and talk to the neighbors. We forgot to do that yesterday," Tina adds.

You can see Jack's brain working. Outings to a wild place like the bluff aren't his sort of thing, but he doesn't want Tina to get mad at him again. "Sure," he says to her with a smile.

Diane Rivers has been watching all of you. "Tina, dear," she says. "What kind of nail polish is that?"

Tina holds it out for her to see. "Corpuscle."

Diane peers at it. "How interesting. Halloween's in two days, isn't it? Tuesday night. Is anyone getting dressed up?"

Heads are shaken all around. "Candace wants me to go trick-or-treating with Eve," you tell them.

"I guess you're a little old for costumes," Diane says.

"Yeah, but there's supposed to be a killer party at Nadir's house," Tina says.

Jack groans. "Don't tell me—Nadir is a Shadow, right?"

Tina winks. "You're all invited. You can come with me."

"Okay, but I'm bringing plenty of garlic," Jack quips.

* * *

Later that afternoon, you head down to the beach with Randy. With the threatening weather, not many surfers are out. Plus, the storm has generated a monster swell. The waves are big, big in a way that produces a hollow pit in your stomach.

A smattering of surfers stand around in their wetsuits, watching the terrifying waves crash. "Check out them mackers," one guy says. "And it's only low tide."

Among the surfers, you see a head that's a familiar color blond. It belongs to a ruddy-faced guy, maybe 21, with long hair, a big chest, and big arms. You're pretty sure he's the surfer you're looking for.

You motion Randy over near the guy. "Hey," you say loudly, "did anyone hear about a surfer that disappeared out around Devil's Rack a couple of days ago?"

Heads shake all around. But then one boy turns to the blond surfer. "Didn't I see you paddling out there, Kirk?"

"Wasn't me, bro." Kirk doesn't look at you, but stares fixedly out to sea. That's not unusual. You're carrying a bodyboard, so surfers often pretend you don't exist. And Kirk looks like the most serious of serious surfers.

"Hey *sponger*," a kid calls behind you. "You're supposed to be some kind of detective, aren't you? Well, you sure screwed up on that Mandrake house, huh? Guess you were seeing things."

You whirl around and recognize Trip Cabot's buzz cut. He waggles his fingers. "Seeing ghosts? *Wooo-oooo*."

People laugh all around you.

"My dad's going to build a golf course out there," he goes on. "You can visit me—if you can afford it."

Randy draws himself up in front of Trip. "You're pretty proud of yourself, aren't you? Like you actually did something of your own."

Trip gives a self-satisfied smile. "All I'm saying is that your mother can save her energy. That place is history, and I don't mean the landmark kind."

Suddenly, Kirk stands beside Randy. "You're full of it," he tells Trip. Then, he fixes on you. "And you're a fool if you go prowling around that place. Take it from me."

"You don't know as much as my dad—" Trip starts.

But Kirk just shoves him aside. He trots down to the water, jumps on his board, and starts paddling out

Randy eyes Trip. "So your dad found an heir, huh?"

You see the surprise register on Trip's face before he narrows his eyes to wonder how Randy got the information.

"Come on," Randy says to you. He marches toward the waves. "We'll see who's living out there a year from now," he calls over his shoulder to Trip.

"Yeah, we'll *see*," Trip shoots back from shore.

Randy jumps on his surfboard, and you hop on your bodyboard. You have to duck down under a couple of monster waves to get out. It seems to take them forever to pass over your head. Each time you come to the surface with relief, as you hear them crash behind you.

When you finally get out beyond the breaks, you glance around for Kirk but he's nowhere to be seen.

Randy sits up on his board. His arm shoots out to the north. "There! He's heading for Devil's Rack again!"

You push yourself up and catch a glimpse of Kirk's blond head. "You don't think we should…"

"Come on!" Randy says.

You start kicking and paddling after Kirk. At first you don't think about what you're doing, because you're just trying to keep up with Randy. The farther you go, though, the more frightened you feel. You've never been this far from land on your board. Not only that, but as you progress to the north, the shore becomes a wall of rocks. You remind yourself that with the tide low, there must be a little bit of beach left.

Now you see jagged rock haystacks surround you. You've entered Devil's Rack. Waves come from every direction, tossing you from side to side. You never know where the next wave will hit. They're all mixed up because of the rocks. You feel as if you're caught in some kind of giant washing machine. You gasp furiously, from fear as much as from exertion. With the clouds lowering on the horizon, the light has become murky and dim. It seems entirely possible that you could be swallowed up out here without a trace.

You don't like this. You don't like it at all.

But you have no choice but to go forward. Randy isn't stopping, and you can't go back alone.

Most of the waves are charging in toward the rock wall of the bluff now. They begin to push you toward shore. But every once in a while, a wave breaks back off the rocks and smacks you in the face. You're starting to wonder how you're going to land safely, when Randy tacks around to paddle beside you.

"Hold on to my leash," he commands.

You grab the cord that connects his leg to the back of the board. Randy swims hard for shore and guides his surfboard along the rolling waves. You hold on for your life. A big one rises up and pitches you in the direction of a big boulder on the narrow strip of shore. Randy cuts his board along the wave, managing to avoid the rock. You're deposited on the little bit of sand uncovered by the low tide.

Randy helps you to your feet. You drag yourself and your board out of reach of the raging waves.

"Where's Kirk?" you gasp.

"He couldn't have gone far."

"Unless he got eaten by the waves."

A reassuring smile breaks out on Randy's face. "That was pretty wild, huh?"

You just shake your head. You notice something in the sand. "Here we go. Footprints."

Randy tucks your boards behind some rocks. Still wearing your wetsuit, booties, and gloves, you follow the footprints a short way along the beach. They disappear at a series of rock benches that step up the side of the bluff. You spot some dark spaces in between the benches. Randy sees them, too.

"Caves," he says. "Let's check them out."

"But," you sputter, "we don't have any investigation tools. We don't even have a flashlight."

"We'll just look for a minute," Randy insists. "If we need to go back for a flashlight, we will."

"All right," you agree. "But let's hurry. It's going to be dark soon."

You pick your way up the rock benches until you come to the biggest cave. Its mouth yawns wide and dark. You enter.

Begin your investigation of the caves on the Digital Detectives web site:

http://www.ddmysteries.com
and enter the key phrase **CAVES**

When you've finished this investigation, the web site will give you a page number to return to.

When you get back outside of the cave, you see the disappointed look on Randy's face.

"It was pretty dark in there," you say.

Randy nods. "Yeah."

Both of you stand silently while the sun sinks over the horizon. You can tell Randy doesn't feel good about leaving.

"I wonder where Kirk went to," you offer.

Randy folds his arms. "He's got to be in the cave. I don't see where else he could have gone."

"Let's just check around first, okay?" you say. "If we don't see any signs of him, then we go back into the cave."

"Deal," Randy agrees.

You hunt around the narrow beach underneath the bluff for more clues about Kirk. The only thing you find is his surfboard, tucking into a rock crevice near the cave.

"He's got to be inside," Randy says.

Reluctantly you nod in agreement. You follow Randy into the mouth of the cave once again, hoping you'll find more this time.

 Return to the cave on the
Digital Detectives web site:

http://www.ddmysteries.com
and enter the key phrase **CAVESTRY**

When you've finished this investigation, the
web site will give you a page number to
return to.

8
THE INITIATORS

Your flashlight beam crosses Craig's face, revealing both anguish and anger. You have a million questions to ask him—like just how did he end up living, against his will, it seems, in this cave? And is he telling the truth about why Kirk the surfer is lying unconscious with his head bashed open?

But the questions will have to wait. Right now, you need to get Craig out of the cave.

Randy checks Kirk again. "He's not bleeding, and his breathing is regular. He should be all right until a rescue crew can get down here."

You bring a blanket from Craig's bed to keep Kirk warm. Then, you and Randy each grasp one of Craig's arms and legs. Gripping the flashlight between your teeth, you carry him in a sitting position to the mouth of the cave. It's not easy. Half the time, Craig gripes at you for not keeping him upright, and half the time, he tells you how glad he is to be taken out of there.

When you get outside, it's almost too dark to see. You manage to get Craig onto Randy's surfboard. Randy uses his leash to tie Craig to the board. Craig grips the edges tightly. Then you and Randy pick him up and carry him up the narrow trail. The way is muddy, and several times you come close to losing your footing in your neoprene booties.

"Careful!" Craig commands, as if you're some kind of porter. Somehow you manage to keep him on the board.

After the first few minutes, your arms ache so badly that it feels as if they're about to fall off. You have to take lots of rests, which means setting Craig down in a precarious position. The ocean roars ominously below, only the white foam is visible in the dying light. It's a nerve-rattling-enough climb for you. You can't really blame Craig for being tense.

When you have finally reached the top, you set the board down with a huge sigh of relief. Randy loosens the leash so that Craig can sit up. His face is a little less strained.

"Thanks for carrying me up." He gives a bitter laugh. "Going down was easier. Kirk carried me on his back."

"So, it was Kirk who put you in the cave?" Randy asks.

"Yeah." He stops and looks you and Randy up and down. "How come all you people out here wear those space suits?"

You look down at yourself. "You mean our wetsuits? We wear these so we can swim in the ocean. The water's cold."

"Huh. Well, they're pretty freaky. Everything out here is. That creepy house and all the stuff that goes on in there."

You regard Craig's features in the dim light. Although he's slight, you figure he must be 17 or 18 years old. His face is curiously old and young at the same time. There's a toughness in it, a haunted look that seems out of place for someone his age. But he also seems very innocent and vulnerable.

"So you were living in the Mandrake house before the cave?" Randy asks.

"Yeah, it was pretty sweet for a while," Craig answers. "All the food, videos, and comics I wanted. Anything I asked for. Until that guy came back again."

Before you can ask what guy, and why he was in the

Mandrake house in the first place, Craig holds his hand out and groans. "Oh no. Just what we don't need."

The first drops of rain have begun to fall. The storm is here.

"Okay, let's move," Randy orders. "We'll carry you to the Mandrake house to get out of the rain, then go for help."

Craig lies down on the surfboard again, Randy straps him in, and you set off toward the house. You have to circle around the big iron fence to get to the front gate.

As you pause to open the gate, Craig looks up at the house with what appears to be longing. Then a shadow seems to cross his face. His expression of hope morphs into a mask of fear.

"What is it?" you ask.

Craig's lips barely move. "I hope the fiends don't come tonight."

"Fiends?" Randy asks, puzzled.

Craig nods. He's not joking. But the rain starts to pound harder, so you've got to keep moving. Once you get Craig out of the rain on the porch, you run around the side of the house and go for the dog door.

Bonk! Your head hits something hard as you try to get through. Someone has blocked the entry!

You dash back to the porch. Just as you get there, a white streak flashes over the landscape. A tremendous crack and a roar comes out of the sky. You cringe. Randy does too. Craig lets out a little wail.

"Don't worry," Randy tells him. "We're safe here."

But Craig, propped up on an elbow, is staring toward the gate, his eyes wide with fear. "No, we're not."

You peer into the darkness. A shiver goes down your spine.

Craig's fear is contagious.

Then, it happens. Another flash, another crack. And in the moment of the flash, outlined starkly in the white landscape, is a human figure. Though you only see him for a split second, his after-image etches in your mind. Tall, wearing a trench coat and hat, shoulders square against the rain, walking toward the house.

"It's him!" Craig cries. "The man who's after me. That's why they had to hide me in the house, because of him!"

"Is he one of the fiends?" you ask.

Craig is trying to scramble to his feet. "I don't know. All I know is, he's the one who's looking for me. Get me out of here—now!"

"Hold on, Craig—" Randy begins.

You hear the gate open. Craig starts to drag himself across the porch. You and Randy help him up, before he rolls down the stairs. He throws an arm over each of your shoulders, and you half-drag him into the bushes on the left side of the house.

A moment later you hear the sound of shoes on the porch stairs. There's a pause, and then a voice. "Who's there?"

You recognize the voice. It's Carlos, the man from Mexico City. The three of you remain still as stones. Rain drips down behind your ear. Craig is shaking.

After a long pause, you hear something like keys. But the door doesn't open right away. Carlos fumbles with the keys for several minutes, before he finally gives an exclamation of satisfaction. The door opens, then closes again.

Randy tries to reason with Craig. "We've got to get you out of the rain. My friend and I have our wetsuits on, so we'll be okay. But you need to be inside."

"I'm not going in. Not with him there," Craig states.

"But the nearest house is half a mile down the road," Randy insists. "I don't think we can carry you that far."

"We'll just stay here." A flash of lightning illuminates Craig's face. You can see the resolution in it. So you and Randy just sigh and stand with Craig in the rain, trying to get a little protection from the vines on the side of the house.

After a minute, Randy has an idea. He runs up to the porch, adjusts the lock on the inside of the door, then returns.

Half an hour later, the door opens again and Carlos leaves. You wait until you're sure that he's gone. Then, you help Craig up the steps. Randy's trick works: the door remained unlocked. The first thing you do inside is to find an old candlestick and some matches to give yourself more light.

Craig insists on being taken upstairs to his old room. "I don't want the fiends to find me," he says.

Craig is very determined, so you and Randy help him up the stairs. You're almost afraid to ask, but you can't resist. "Who are these fiends?"

Craig's lip quivers. "A cult, maybe. They chant, and I can smell fire when they're here."

You recall the ashes in the fireplace and the burned things among them. By now, you're feeling just as nervous as Craig. He sees this and says, "Don't worry, they stay downstairs."

Great, you think. That's really reassuring.

Once Craig is settled on the mattress of his old bed, Randy says that he'll go to the farmhouse down the road to summon help.

"All right," you agree. "But make it fast—please."

Randy nods. He picks up the flashlight, leaving you and Craig in the room with a single candle burning.

Craig lies back on the bed. His good foot shakes nervously, bringing a steady squeak from the bedsprings. A gust of wind rattles the windows. The candle flickers. The whole house seems to creak and sway on its foundations. You cup your hands over the candle flame, protecting it, as though it is life itself.

Craig breathes heavily and stares at the ceiling. You watch him out of the corner of your eye for a minute, trying to imagine what it must have been like to live in that cave for two days, helpless to leave. You can't believe that anyone would do something like that to him. But it's even more amazing that Craig doesn't seem more traumatized by the experience than he is. How did he keep his sanity?

"So," you say to him, "how did you end up in that cave?"

"Back in Texas, I got hit by a car," Craig explains. "That's what broke my leg. Anyway, I was minding my own business in the hospital when—"

He's interrupted by a loud banging. You stare at each other. You're anxious to hear the rest of Craig's story, so you say, "Maybe it's just a shutter."

But the banging comes again. And again. The entire house shudders. Someone, or something, is trying to get in.

Craig's face goes white as cheese. "The fiends."

Your mouth turns to dry dust. The banging continues, fierce and deliberate. It's not the wind.

Then, it stops. Next, you hear some shuffling downstairs. Another bolt of lightning strikes. The flash bursts into the room, and for a moment, you see your own shadow cast against the wall like some ghostly double that has come for you. You actually jump away from it in fear.

When the rumble of thunder stops, new sounds come from downstairs. Several voices chant mysterious syllables in a creepy monotone. In spite of yourself, you move toward the door. You glance back at Craig, who remains frozen with fear on the bed.

You creep out of the room and peer down the main stairs. The entry way is lit by dancing flames. A procession of shrouded figures file through, carrying lit torches. Glinting eyes flicker here and there under the hoods.

They proceed solemnly through the door and into the living room. You continue down the stairs, as silently as you can. Your heart thumps so hard that you're afraid the fiends can hear it.

From the entry hall, you spy on the group. Seven of them are gathered around a giant blaze in the fireplace. The room is alight with flames.

Someone brings forward an object held in upturned arms. It appears to be some kind of offering. The figure turns, and now you see what it is. Something large, wet and pink skewered on a wooden spit. The spit is placed over the fire. The chanting rises again, and you can't make yourself stop watching. The offering sizzles over the flames. You try to stifle a choking sound in your throat.

One of the figures turns. You've been spotted! You back away.

Too late! They all see you now.

A voice comes from behind one of the hoods. "Violator! Only the initiated may see this!

"You must be initiated," another voice commands. "The initiation of fire."

You recognize the voice. "Mordar!" you cry. "It's me! Tina's friend!"

He doesn't respond. Another figure lights a torch in the fire. He begins to advance on you, followed by the others.

"Sorrow!" you plead. "Don't do this!"

But their eyes are fixed on you. The chain letter flashes into your mind. Your four days are up. You remember Mordar and Sorrow sabotaging Danny's bike. Have they somehow contrived to get you here in order to make their prophecy come true? Impossible! Yet they keep advancing on you.

Suddenly, a thump-thump-thumping sounds from above. "Tibias!" a Shadow cries. "You have come!"

They all freeze, staring up at the ceiling.

This is your chance. You break for the door. Some of the Shadows rush at you, grasping at your wetsuit. But it still has a little rain on it. Their hands slip off. You fling open the door and flee into the night.

* * *

You don't know how far down the road you've fled, before you're able to look back without seeing torch lights in pursuit. You've fallen several times, smearing your wetsuit with mud. You've also nearly been stopped by a pang of guilt for leaving Craig behind. But you know that you're no match for the seven Shadows. For both Craig and you to have any hope, you need to get help.

Now you walk blindly, invisible in the dark. So, the Shadows are Craig's fiends, you think. How much weirder is this night going to get?

The rain comes down with new force, as if trying to

punish everything below. Even though it pounds the top of your head, the rest of your body, inside the wetsuit, is protected. This must be what it's like to be a seal, you think.

The mud slowly washes off under the pounding rain. You walk carefully, knowing that if you sprain an ankle in a pothole, you could be stuck out here for the night.

Where is Randy? you wonder. You should have run into him by now.

Then you *do* run into something. But it's not Randy. It's a large hulking object. You jump away, then realize it's not alive. It's a car, parked on the side of the road. Very cautiously you make your way past it.

You pass a dark building on the left, which you remember seeing in the daylight. A little farther down the road, a welcome light appears. It's the farmhouse. At last. The cozy warmth coming from inside the house is about the most welcome sight in the world right now.

You knock on the door. A white-haired man answers it. "What are you doing out in this rain?" he asks with concern.

"I need some help," you tell him. "Can I use your phone?"

He motions you in. "Martha," he calls into another room, "we need another towel!"

You wait while Martha brings you a towel to dry off with. The man's name is Howard. They bring you into the kitchen, where the phone is. You call Tina and tell her to send her dad to the Mandrake house immediately with an ambulance. You also ask her to call Candace and let her know you're all right.

"Can't talk," you reply to Tina's questions. "I'm using someone else's phone."

Martha puts a cup of steaming chocolate in your hand.

"Come on into the living room," Howard says. "You're our second visitor tonight! The other fellow's car got stuck in the mud."

You stop dead at the entrance to the living room. Carlos sits on the sofa.

He stares at you for a moment, then knits his brows. "Tell me, is it a good night for surfing?"

You quickly turn and hand the mug back to Martha. "I've got to be going."

"You should stay inside," Martha protests.

"Thanks a lot!" you say, heading for the door.

Carlos springs to his feet. "Wait!"

You don't. You open the door and race back out into the rain. A glance back shows that Carlos is still framed in the doorway. You hear his voice through the rain, but you can't make out what he's saying.

Soon the warm lights of the farmhouse are out of sight. You're alone again in the night.

You walk back in the direction of the Mandrake house, not knowing what you'll do when you get there. Hide outside the house until help comes, you guess. For a moment, you consider not going back. But you can't leave Craig alone there. And you need to find out what happened to Randy.

A ghostly howl quavers through the night. You walk a little faster. It's just a coyote, you remind yourself.

Finally, you reach the iron gate. Lurid red light flickers from within. You can't help but wonder what the Shadows are doing now. How far do they go with their rites?

You climb up on top of an old wheelbarrow in order to get to a vine-covered window. By parting the greenery, you can peer into the living room.

What you see inside shocks you. The Shadows are on their knees, bowing before the fire and the crest above the mantle. They seem possessed by fear and awe.

Then you hear a voice from somewhere above. "Louder!" the voice brays. "More!"

The Shadows groan and flail around. The voice bellows out again. "You have displeased me! You must leave!"

The Shadows look at each other in confusion. "But Tibias," cries Mordar, "we have not completed our offering."

"BE GONE!"

A great pounding comes from inside. The Shadows rise and move toward the door. You hurry to the corner of the house and watch them exit.

When they have left, all is silent again. Do you dare go inside? Who, or what, did that voice come from?

You think of Craig, upstairs alone. That decides it. You creep through the front door, silent in your wetsuit booties, and mount the stairs. Whatever may be up there, it's your responsibility to check on him.

Besides, there was something familiar about the spirit's voice. You peek into the bedroom. Craig is doubled up on the bed—but in silent laughter, not pain. Standing next to him, with one hand clamped over his mouth, is Randy. In his other hand is a bullhorn.

"There you are!" Randy whispers. "Have the Shadows left?"

"They're gone," you confirm.

Craig and Randy burst out laughing. Randy bows. "Ghost of Tibias Mandrake, at your service."

You gawk. "How did you do it?"

"It was really Craig that started it," Randy explains.

"Yeah," Craig breaks in. "I didn't know that they were kids.

I thought that they were some weird cult, and they might barbecue me if I got caught." He shudders, then looks at you. "I heard you down there crying for help, so I tried to distract them."

"That's what gave me the idea," Randy says. "I overheard the Shadows getting all freaked at Craig's thumping. I looked around a little and found this bullhorn in the master bedroom. That's how I became the voice of Tibias Mandrake."

"But…how did you get back inside?" you ask. "And where have you been, anyway?"

"I was going to ask you the same thing," Randy responds. "I went down the road to that first house. The guy there let me call 911. When I came back, the Shadows were all busy with their rigmarole. It wasn't too hard to slip upstairs."

"Now, I get it," you say. "You must have been inside the first house when I passed by it. I went to the farmhouse and called Tina's dad. Then, I found out that they had another guest—Carlos. His car got stuck in the mud. I didn't wait around to find out what he was doing there."

"Too bad," Randy muses.

"Yeah, maybe I should have stayed," you say. "But I was kind of freaked myself."

"I wouldn't have stayed," Craig states.

"That was so weird—what the Shadows were doing," you say, recalling the scene with a shudder. "What do you think that offering was, that they were burning over the fire?"

"Probably, just something they got at a butcher shop," Randy muses. "I'll bet if we get to the bottom of it, they were just having some fun. Scaring themselves for Halloween."

A light flashes from outside. But this time it's not lightning. "That's the ambulance," you tell Craig. "They'll take you to the hospital and make sure you're all right."

Craig looks worried. "You're not disappearing on me, are you?"

"Don't worry," Randy assures him. "We'll come and visit. We've still got a lot of things to talk about."

"I'll say," you murmur, as you hear Tina's voice calling your name from the bottom of the stairs.

9
INFERNO

You get home about ten o'clock that night. Never have you been so exhausted, and never so glad to see Eve and Candace.

Your sister had refused to go to sleep until you got home. Now that you are, she wants to know everything that you've been doing. Luckily, Candace talks her into going to bed before you have to try to explain. Then, Candace heats up some dinner, which you wolf down. You tell her about rescuing Craig from the cave, but leave out the part about the Shadows and Carlos. You've got a lot more investigation to do, and you don't want her to get so worried that she holds you back.

As you fall into bed, a million questions and images swirl in your mind. The pounding rain, the pounding surf, the pounding of Craig's foot on the bedroom floor. The hooded figures, the lurid flames, all of the people lurking like vultures over the mansion, each more keen than the next to have it for their own. And Craig, so stoic, toughing it out in the cave, and yet so innocent.

What does it all add up to? You're much too tired, and there's too much more work to be to done, to figure it out right now.

The next day, Monday, brings many more questions than answers. The Digital Detectives meet at lunch. You and

Randy get a chance to fill in the others about some of the things that happened out on the bluff last night. But you don't have time to describe everything.

"I'll write up a report, like we did on our last case," you suggest. "I'll tell you all the gory details."

"Excellent idea," Randy agrees. "We should all take assignments, like before. We need to figure out why Craig was being kept in that house, and then moved to the cave. It's outrageous."

"And yet, he didn't seem to realize it," you point out. "That's another mystery...where did he come from?"

"And does he have anything to do with the Mandrake estate," Jack adds. "Did they move him to the cave because the auction was making their little hiding place too hot?"

"I'm going to visit him in the hospital after school," Randy says. "Want to come?"

You want to say yes, but then, you remember what Candace said to you as you left for school. "I can't. Candace made me promise to come home after school. With my parents away, Eve has been upset that I'm gone so much. I've got a lot of homework to catch up on, too."

Randy nods sympathetically. "I'll go with you," Jack volunteers. "I want to see this guy for myself."

"What about you, Tina?" Randy asks. "Have you seen the Shadows today?"

Tina shakes her head. "I wouldn't be totally shocked if they skipped school, if what you're saying about last night is true."

"You've only heard the highlights," you tell her. "It gets better. Or worse, depending on how you see it."

"Well," Tina goes on, "I'll try to find Sorrow this afternoon.

I know I'll see her tomorrow night, at her Halloween party."

"They must be the ones who drew all those symbols on the wall," you note. "They worship Tibias Mandrake or something."

Tina cocks her head. "They can be funny. I never know when they're being serious and when they're putting me on."

"We should find out about Kirk and Carlos, too," you say.

"Precisely," Jack agrees. "So far, all we know is that some weird people are doing weird things out there at the weird house. We're not even sure yet if what was done to Craig is a crime. Maybe he's the criminal, not Kirk."

"Doubt that," Randy says. "But I forgot to tell you, Kirk was rescued from the cave. He's in the hospital, unconscious."

"Okay. All I'm saying is, let's keep our eye on the big picture," Jack continues. "If you take a good hard look at who's got the most at stake here, it's the ones who want that house so badly. We should check out these real estate people. Especially Bill Cabot and Betsy Akers."

"Definitely," Tina agrees. "Follow the money. I'll take Betsy. I can tell she's up to something."

"I'll take Bill, and talk to Rundell again," Randy says.

"I'll handle Carlos and Mandrake," Jack offers.

"I've got to write up what happened last night," you say. "I can also go back to the farmhouse tomorrow and interview Howard and Martha. Maybe they've noticed things going on out there."

"Good," Tina agrees. "They weren't home yesterday."

The bell rings. The lunch hour has passed quickly.

"All right," Randy announces, "let's have the reports done by tomorrow evening. Bill and Betsy are supposed to file their claims about the heirs in the afternoon. We should know what's happening with the house by then."

* * *

It's kind of a relief to have a quiet evening at home for a change. But you keep hoping the phone will ring. You want to find out what the other Digital Detectives have learned.

Just before you go to bed, you discover that that, too, will have to wait. Their e-mails just say that they found out interesting stuff from Craig, but it will be written up in their reports.

You're amazingly tired again when you go to bed. You must still be recovering from the shock of last night. You slip into a deep sleep, the moment you close your eyes.

But when you awake, you are *wide* awake. You're out of bed before you know it. It's the flames. They're all around you again. What are they doing here? You have no time to think. You only know that you must escape. You stumble in the dark toward your window. Then you remember Eve and Candace. You can't leave without them.

As you approach your door, it begins to dawn on you that it is a dream. No flames are licking outside the window. The door is cool to the touch. What's going on?

Opening the door, you go cautiously down the hallway. Eve is sleeping peacefully. Downstairs, you hear Candace snoring through her door. You prowl through the rest of the house, just to make sure. As you peer out the window, you remember the big rain last night. It put out all the wildfires. So why, after everything else, has the fire dream come to haunt you again?

Then you hear it. A distinct and insistent tapping, as if a messenger has come for you. This is no trick of the wind or of your mind. With growing fear, you mount the stairs to your room. That seems to be where the sound is coming from.

You're right. There is a tap-tap-tap at your bedroom window. Have the Shadows tracked you down? Is it the ghost of Tibias Mandrake? You take a deep breath and fling back the curtains. You nearly scream. A face peers through the window at you!

You quickly recover. It's only Randy.

"Open up!" he gestures urgently.

When you do, he tells you to get dressed and get your bike and follow him right away. "It's the Mandrake house."

You dress quickly and sneak out onto the roof with him. As you climb down the tree, you're glad you put on a jacket. The night is cool. You get your bike from the garage and head out in the direction of the bluff.

By the time you get to the turnoff, you can see that the sky is illuminated by some great glow. A feeling of dread overcomes you, as you ride down the paved road, which then turns to dirt. You pull to a stop and stare.

It's the Mandrake mansion. Being consumed by flames.

You look at Randy. Both of you are so stunned, you can't talk. The fire trucks are there, but they've exhausted their supply of water. The firemen are now focused on saving the smaller building near the main house.

You and Randy park your bikes and walk around the trucks and into the front yard. Nothing but a skeleton of the house remains. Its bones are aflame, a giant gridwork of fire. The heat of the blaze sears your skin. You have to stay all the way back along at the iron fence to bear it. The flames lick at the sky like hungry animals, consuming oxygen as fast as they can get it. The roar is overpowering. You feel as if it's about to consume you, too.

Then, as the timbers burn, you begin to hear them creak and groan. They quiver like unsteady legs, then twist, and finally, give up and crash to the ground in a big billow of smoke. It's like watching some great creature die.

You're transfixed by the spectacle. You feel as if you're watching your nightmare come true.

Once the various sections of the house have fallen, the blaze continues to burn. But now, it is spread out at a lower level. The heat has diminished. You're finally able to turn to Randy. You can't believe what you've just witnessed. It was both terrifying and strangely exhilarating.

Only when you see the crushed look on Randy's face do you begin to realize what's been lost.

"This couldn't have been an accident," he says, dazed. "The rain gave everything a thorough soaking on Sunday. All the wildfires are out."

"So someone set it deliberately?"

"Or else caused it by something they were doing inside. It couldn't have been started from the outside. The house and vegetation around it were too wet."

You nod. What Randy says makes sense.

He grabs your arm. "Come on, let's look around."

A cluster of people is standing near the fire trucks. You notice Howard and Martha, pajama pants sticking out from underneath coats. They are talking to two other people, shaking their heads sadly. Then you notice another man, standing by himself near the gate. It's Carlos, in his hat and trench coat. His feet seem rooted to the spot. The flames dance over his skin, giving it a sickly metallic look, crossed by a few smudges of ash.

You edge closer to him, wondering what you might say. Then, you stop abruptly as he lifts his hand and wipes something from his cheek. The light shifts a little bit. Now, you see the wet streaks coming down from his eyes.

You back away, even more unsure what to say to him. Randy sees the same thing you do, and tugs at your sleeve.

You begin to follow him across the singed lawn, but you're stopped by a trio of firemen. "Please stand back," one of them orders. "We're going to need to clear the area."

Other firemen are telling the people near the trucks the same thing. "Come on," Randy says, "let's get out of here, before we get stuck behind a bunch of cars."

You get back on your bikes. Luckily, Randy has a headlamp on his bike, so you can see the road ahead. You ride slowly and silently together. The magnitude of what you have witnessed slowly descends upon you.

You're jolted out of your thoughts by something flashing by you. Your first thought is that it's a deer or coyote. But as you hit the brakes to avoid it, you catch a glimpse of a fiendish human face, its features contorted with fear and horror.

The person vanishes into the brush. You continue riding. Slowly the features of the face register. They were contorted in fear but still you recognize them.

The fiendish face belonged to Sorrow.

10

THE REPORTS: PART ONE

The following morning dawns chilly and gray. You slept restlessly the remainder of the night. No fire dreams haunted you any more. They are far too real now.

Bleary-eyed, you crawl from bed. You haven't had nearly enough sleep, but still your mind is racing. Slowly it has sunk in that the Mandrake house no longer exists. Something that once was there—an imposing structure, an odd and eccentric monument to an odd man—suddenly is not. Poof. Overnight.

How did it happen? Who's responsible? Why did they do it?

These are the questions that you ask when you see the Digital Detectives at lunch time. It is Halloween, and the halls are decorated with orange and black. Kids put on masks and fake blood at lunch. After your experiences on the bluff, it all seems so phony.

"The police don't have a clue," Tina informs you. "My dad said that the place burned so completely that they're unlikely to find evidence. They'll do a full investigation, of course. The one thing they're sure of is that the fire started inside the house."

"The electricity and gas are off, so those couldn't have been the source," Randy says. "That only leaves a human cause." He shakes his head and stares off into space. "I can't believe it happened. My mom is just in shock. She was walking around like a zombie this morning."

"Yeah, it must be really hard for her," Tina sympathizes. "All that work she put in."

"It's up to us," Randy decides, pushing a lock of hair off his forehead. "At this point, we know more than anyone else about the Mandrake house and the people around it. We're in the best position to solve the crime. Who was keeping Craig locked up in a cave, and why? And who started the fire?"

"And are they related?" you add. "What did you find out from visiting Craig?"

"*Lots*," Randy answers. "He's doing fine. There's so much to tell, though, I should just write it up."

"Yes," Jack says quickly. "Let's do this in an orderly way. We should all write up our reports and read them tonight. I think we've all got some more investigating to do, too."

"Yeah, I couldn't find Sorrow yesterday," Tina says. "If that was really her you saw on the bluff last night. I'll talk to her tonight at her party. You guys can come, too."

"Pass," Jack says.

"Not me," you add. "I don't need to see any more burning torches coming at me."

"Okay," Tina says, looking down. She seems disappointed, like maybe this is not a party she wants to go to by herself. You glance at her hands. She's not wearing any nail polish today. Maybe she's back to being the regular old Tina, you think.

"So we'll see everyone's reports tonight?" Jack says.

"Right," Randy agrees, standing up. "I'll be down at the courthouse this afternoon to find out what Mr. Rundell plans to do, now that there's nothing but a bunch of ashes for sale."

✳ ✳ ✳

After school, you make a trip out to the farmhouse where Howard and Martha live. After talking with them, you hurry home for dinner before it gets dark. You've already started writing your report, about the night you found Craig. Once you finish that, you'll write up your visit with Howard and Martha.

But first you help Eve get ready for Halloween. She dresses up as a tiger. You let her chase you around the house, pretending that you're afraid of being eaten. Then, you take her out trick-or-treating. It's fun to see the other little kids. You remember what it was like to live in the fantasy world of being another creature for the night. To be scary and a little bit scared, but not creepy. Just for a moment, you envy Eve. Being six years old suddenly looks like fun.

After Eve has gone to bed, you sit down to finish your report. Then, you check your e-mail for the others' reports. So far, Jack's and Randy's have arrived.

YOUR REPORT

Howard and Martha were happy to see me. They couldn't understand why I ran away the other night. There was no need to fear Carlos, they said. He was just a nice gentleman who happened to get his rental car stuck in the mud. He told them that he's a lawyer who's worried about the fate of the house, but he wants to keep a low profile. In fact, he once was good friends with Tibias Mandrake. If all that is true, it

93

would explain his tears while he watched the house burn.

They also told me a little about Mandrake. The bluff used to be a quiet farm and ranching scene before he built his mansion. Then, things got a little weird. They were too polite to say so, but it seems like his impact on their lives was not all for the good. But they still said that he was always very courteous and helpful, when needed. He kept to himself, except when he would ask permission to dig on their property for some prehistoric bone.

RANDY'S REPORT

County Courthouse: I went down there this afternoon. I can't believe this guy Rundell. I'd like to pop him one. He gave me this little smile when I asked him about the Mandrake house, almost like he was glad it burned down.

He said, "It's always been the property that's of real value anyway, not the house. The house was, perhaps, a liability. Now, with the historical angle out of the way, the property is clear for development."

Then, the smile again. "Tell your mother that I'm sorry about this." As if he really cares.

"What about the fire?" I asked. "What if it's arson?"

"The police will do their investigation, of course," he said. "But it could take a long time. I see no reason to delay the sale more than a day or two. It's not productive. Besides, I understand that Bill Cabot is going to file some papers that may make the auction moot. Perhaps, Betsy Akers, too."

"What do you know about them?" I asked.

"They're both fine businessmen—people. I think either one would do an excellent job with the property. On

Thursday afternoon, I'll be showing the property to prospective buyers. The remains of the house are, of course, off limits. But really, it is the eighty acres of land that we want to inspect more closely."

"Why did you give my mom the wrong key for the last tour?"

Rundell's face got red. "I gave her the right key. I tested it myself later. Someone had changed the lock. Perhaps your mother herself?"

I pointed out that she would have had the right key if it was her. Then I asked, "Doesn't that make you suspicious that something was going on in the house?"

His eyes narrowed at me. "Obviously. But you don't have to look very far to find it. It's either that little satanic group with the black fingernails—or it's you and your little group. I told the police to investigate you both."

I have to admit this stunned me a little. I made the mistake of saying that we were conducting an investigation of our own. Then, he told me to get out of his office.

BUT, as I was leaving, I saw Bill Cabot come walking down the hall in his golf clothes, along with some guy in a suit. I decided just to go for it. I asked Mr. Cabot if he had an heir to the Mandrake estate on his side.

He's a smooth guy. He covered up his surprise pretty well. He changed the subject and went on about how sorry he was about the fire, my mother, blah blah blah fake stuff.

I said, "I guess her bad luck is your good fortune."

"No, no, no, I'd never wish for such a thing. It's a terrible thing that happened, *tragic*. I'd rather win fair and square." Then, he had the nerve to wink at me. "Which I would have anyway. Say, your father's a golfer, isn't he?"

As a matter of fact, he is.

"I think that he'll enjoy the course," Cabot said. "It'll be world class."

What I should have said was, "You know very well that we could never afford to join your club, you two-faced phony." What I did, instead, was smile and nod and then ask if Betsy also was going to make a claim.

This stopped him in his tracks. But like I said, he's smooth. He stroked his Adam's apple and said, "I hear Betsy's been delayed. Maybe she never had anyone to begin with. She's a good bluffer, you know."

At that point the guy in the suit, who I guess is a lawyer, said, "If you'll excuse us, we need to deliver these papers before business hours are over."

Hospital: I visited Craig there two times, yesterday afternoon and today, after I saw Rundell and Cabot. Craig's spirits are amazingly good. He does also enjoy the attention that the nurses give him for surviving such an unusual situation.

The police make him nervous, though. We're the only ones he seems willing to confide in. In fact, he hasn't yet told anyone else that he had a disturbing visitor today. Another guy was involved in keeping him in the house. Drew. Craig told me that Kirk is the main one he remembers, but Drew was around, too. About Kirk's age, but with brown hair and gray eyes.

Anyway, according to Craig, Drew came in to warn him that he was still in big danger and that he should come away with him, as soon as he could leave. Craig didn't trust him because of the cave, and told him so. Drew kept insisting. He said that the cave was the only safe place at the time. Safe from *what*? Craig asked him. From the bad men, Drew said. I guess this worked on Craig before, but it's not any more.

Drew kept pressing it, Craig said. Didn't Craig know that Carlos was hunting for him around that very night, last night? That proves that they were right to move Craig to the cave in the first place. Drew made it sound like it's more than just Carlos now. Craig said that he wondered why the story kept changing. Then, Drew changed the subject and started laying a guilt trip on Craig for almost killing Kirk. Did he know that he'd put Kirk in a coma and he might never wake up? That'd be murder! Is this how he treats a guy he owes his life to?

Obviously, we need to check out this Drew guy. This is major news.

By the way, what Drew said about Kirk is exaggerated. It's true that Kirk is unconscious, but the doctors expect him to recover.

Jack also visited Craig with me yesterday and is writing a report about him.

✳ ✳ ✳

You move on to Jack's report. But your head starts to droop as you read it. You haven't been getting enough sleep lately, and you're exhausted. What you need is some sleep so that you'll be fresh when you read the other two reports in the morning. You shut down your computer, climb into bed, and you're asleep before you know it.

11
THE REPORTS: PART TWO

You wake up early so that you'll have time to read Jack's report. With relief, you see that Tina's has also arrived. You check the time stamp. She sent it at 12:24 a.m. She had a late night!

JACK'S REPORT
Case 1: Craig Wheeler
   History: A peculiar and touching case. Male, 18 years old. Suffers from broken leg. This injury was sustained in his former home of Dallas, Texas. He was living on the street and got run over by a car. Prior to his life on the street, he had been under the care of various social agencies and foster homes. He was an orphan. When he turned 18, of legal age, the agency told him that it lacked funds for him and that he would have to take care of himself from that day on. Clearly, he had no preparation for doing so.
   He was tracked down at the hospital, in Texas, by Kirk and Drew. They said that they were working for someone who promised to set him up for life, if he would come to Crescent Bay. Money, material goods, and general well-being were pledged. Very little was required in return, just to sign a paper or two. He was a special person, they told him.
   When he arrived, he was lodged in the old Mandrake house. He was told that this was necessary for his own safe-

ty. A "bad" man (who we now know to be Carlos) was also looking for him. He even agreed to be moved to the cave, when he was told that the house was no longer safe. Kirk promised that he could leave soon, and that soon he would meet his benefactor, who would give him everything he wanted.

However, after two days in the cave, Craig began to think that something was wrong. He tried to get Kirk to take him out, but Kirk kept telling him to wait. Finally, Craig decided he couldn't take it any more. It was too creepy being trapped in the cave. He surprised Kirk by hitting him in the head with a rock on Sunday afternoon. Shortly thereafter, he was rescued by the Digital Detectives.

Symptoms: Craig seems to have had no way to judge the story given to him by Kirk and Drew. But he was happy to go along with it, because he was being given things that no one had ever given him before. Kirk and Drew were the first ones to act as if they cared about him in any way. He did find it strange to live alone in the house, especially when the "fiends" came. But this was no stranger than his whole life story up to that point. The poor fellow had no basis of comparison for what to expect out of life.

Diagnosis: As noted by other detectives, Craig is a strange mixture: street-hardened on one hand, naive and innocent on the other. He has become somewhat more suspicious of what people tell him, since the cave incident. The hopes he had from Kirk for a life of comfort are now dashed. He has no money, and appears to have no family, at least none that he knows of. The few friends that he had in Dallas could not be relied upon for help. When he is released from the local hospital, he has no idea where he will go or how he will live.

Plan of Treatment: He will not give the police his full story. He refuses to press charges against Kirk and Drew. Indeed, since he went along with their scheme, it is not clear that any crime was committed.

Apparently, Carlos Ramirez also attempted to interview Craig this morning. Needless to say, Craig wouldn't speak to him. The nurses kept Carlos out.

However, the Digital Detectives have gained his trust. We must find out what was behind the plot to bring him here, and what relation it has to the Mandrake house and its destruction.

Prognosis: Unknown at this time. If the Digital Detectives succeed in solving this case, there may be some hope for Craig. Otherwise, he may find himself on the street again.

Case 2: Carlos Ramirez

History: Research on the Web shows that Carlos Ramirez was born in Mexico City in 1942. He received degrees from the National University there and from UCLA. He now resides in Los Angeles, where he maintains a law practice.

Symptoms: He has made himself the object of suspicion by lurking about in a trench coat and refusing to reveal the purpose of his presence. He was reported to have been weeping at the sight of the Mandrake house burning.

Diagnosis: Some not entirely legal research into his recent credit card charges was required in order determine his current whereabouts. I telephoned him at the Bayview Hotel and identified myself as an investigator. He was polite enough. He said that he had a personal interest in the Mandrake estate and in seeing it preserved. He was devastated by the destruction of the house. He intends to see to it that those who are responsible are brought to justice. In the meantime, he will reveal new information about the disposition of the estate at his next meeting with Rundell. He would not reveal the nature of the information.

Prognosis: To the extent that I was able to independently confirm his statements, he appears to be telling the truth. However, he bears watching.

Case 3: Tibias Mandrake

History: The man, at the heart of it all, remains a mystery. Little information about him exists on the Internet. The following anecdotal evidence has been received through Randy's web site in answer to his question: "What do you know about Tibias Mandrake?"

"Tibias Mandrake was an amateur paleontologist who made a find very early in his career. He owned the most extensive collection of fossilized animal excrement in the state."

"Mandrake was a first-class crackpot. He kept claiming to find this or that missing link in evolution. He'd dig up some rabbit or deer bone in his back yard and send it to the Smithsonian Institution. Once, he sent them a mud-crusted G.I. Joe doll, as evidence of prehistoric culture on his land. Later on, he turned very weird, claiming he was going to be able to re-animate old bones."

"Tibias Mandrake originally hailed from Bavaria. He lived in St. Louis for a time before coming to Crescent Bay. He was quite a 'Renaissance man', learned in many fields. He could quote an entire speech from Shakespeare, then turn around and recount the latest discovery in human evolution."

"What a pest. He came into my cafe at least once a week.

There's only one thing he would drink. Warm water—at just a certain temperature, mind you—with lemon and honey. Said it was good for the bowels. There was also only one brand of cigarette, which he would smoke, some French type. He made me order them special. Then, he would light up right inside the cafe. Well, that's against the law. I'd have to tell him to smoke outside. Every time, he'd do it. He'd light it up, and I'd make him go outside."

Diagnosis: His peculiar collection speaks for itself. However, even amateurs do get lucky now and again.

Prognosis: In spite of what the Shadows may believe, I contend Tibias Mandrake is safely deceased.

TINA'S REPORT

So, Sorrow's party is all right. Then again, I can only walk around looking morbid for so long. I know for a fact that Sorrow and Mordar are capable of laughter. But the way that they act at the party, you'd think that their smile muscles had gotten injured. I guess it's because it's Halloween.

Plus, they're pretty shaken up. I get there early to talk to them. They act pretty normal before everyone else arrives. They admit, naturally, they were at the Mandrake house two nights ago. Doing their rituals and all. They're just all into the Mandrake lore. FYI: They say that they weren't serious about the torch. But they were going to pretend like they were, right up to the last second.

It's pretty funny to hear them talk about the voice of Tibias Mandrake. You can tell that they think there's probably some explanation for it, but they're not sure what it is (someday, maybe I'll tell them what really happened). See, they do all their hocus pocus and stuff, but all the same, it's sort of a joke to them. I happen to know that they're smart kids and they get good grades.

Then, just when I get around to asking them about the house burning down, people start showing up for the party. All of a sudden Sorrow and Mordar's faces change and go all corpse-like. I can't get another word out of them, for the rest of the night. I guess they can't show anything real around their friends.

I don't stick around for much of the party, to be honest. Except one thing does happen. Trip Cabot and a couple of his friends show up. They've come to make fun of the Shadows. Trip's all like, "Hey, good job burning down that Mandrake house. Now, that it's out of the way my dad can build his clubhouse there."

So, some dude in a hockey mask advances on them with a pitchfork. It's pretty funny to see how those three boys "turn tail and runî.

Betsy Akers: Talk about scary. She doesn't need any black lipstick or Gravedigger nail polish. She's scary all by herself.

I visit her, yesterday afternoon, in her office. You'd think there'd be all kinds of activity going on there, with her big clients and all, but actually it's pretty quiet. There are a lot of boxes, and just one computer set up at Betsy's desk. She looks like she's pulling her hair out when I come in.

I try to be polite, but she totally treats me like I'm some kid getting in her way. So, forgetting about the fact that actually, that's exactly what I am, I get her attention by laying a little 411 on her. I let it slip about the spirit of Tibias haunting the house and how's an heir going to feel about the fact that it burned down?

She demands right away to know what I knew. I tell her that information is "a two-way streetî. She starts threatening to have me arrested for setting the fire. I say that I've got a great alibi, how about you?

I figure that I'm about to get kicked out, but the phone rings. Her face gets all serious. "Yes, I've got the papers," she says. "Can't you wait another day? I just have to get some things squared away."

The other line talks. "Really?" she says. "He filed today? What's the name on that? Mandrake. All right. Yes, I know he'll get priority. Thank you for letting me know, Mr. Rundell. I'll see you Thursday morning."

Well, I put some things together and say, "So, Bill Cabot filed the papers for his heir. What's happening with yours?"

She's startled. It's like she forgot I was there. "What do you know about him?" she asks.

I said not much—yet. Then her voice gets more friendly and she wants to know about the Shadows. Like aren't they interesting and all. I say, yeah, they were the ones who talked to the spirit of Tibias Mandrake, just to see how she reacts.

She's all happy, which surprises me. I thought she'd get all weirded out about it. Instead, she stands up and starts getting ready to leave. "Isn't that interesting," she coos. Like she believes this stuff. What am I saying, duh, she's probably got a coven of her own.

You print the reports, then get yourself ready for school. The Digital Detectives don't have a chance to all meet together, until lunch time again. There, you try to hash out the results of the reports.

"So, who are our main suspects?" Randy asks.

"Let's review the case first," Jack suggests. "Start at the beginning. This all started because of a supposedly lost surfer. It turns out that he wasn't really lost. It was Kirk sneaking over to Devil's Rack to check on Craig in the cave. But why was he keeping Craig there? We don't know yet, and we can't ask Kirk because he's still unconscious."

"But obviously there's somebody who Kirk and Drew are working for," you point out. "Someone with enough money to send them to Dallas to pick up Craig. And to offer Craig all kinds of goodies to keep him happy. We still don't know why."

"Okay, so that's one mystery," Jack says. "The second one, which we're still not sure is connected, is who burned down the Mandrake house, and why."

"Now, we can talk about suspects," Tina says. "We need to think about three things. Motive, means, and opportunity. Who's got the biggest motive? If you ask me, it's one of those real estate people: Bill Cabot or Betsy Akers. By destroying the house, they get the historical society out of their way. The land can be developed."

"Maybe even Rundell," Randy adds. "He sure didn't seem to mind that it went up in flames."

"Right. He could be in league with someone else. But we'd need to find evidence of that to consider him," Jack says.

"We should consider Carlos too," Tina says. "Maybe he was just pretending to be sad about the fire."

"We don't know much about him, that's for sure," you agree. "And he keeps turning up."

"We're leaving out one obvious set of suspects," Jack states. "The Shadows. We know they had the means. They made big fires in the living room. We know that they had the opportunity. Sorrow was seen out there that night."

"But what's missing is the motive," Tina counters. "Why would they burn it down, if they're so into Mandrake?"

"Remember their chain letter," Randy answers. "Remember them sabotaging Danny's bike. Maybe they were trying to make one of their prophecies come true, by torching the house."

Tina shakes her head. "I don't think they would."

"They still could have caused it by accident," Jack says.

"And don't forget about having the means," Randy adds. "If the fire was started inside, it was done either by someone who had a key, or someone who could get through the dog door. It's obvious that one of the Shadows could."

Tina gives a reluctant nod. "So what do we do? What we really need to know is who hired Kirk and Drew. How do we do that?"

The table is silent. No one has an answer.

Jack finally offers his opinion. "That's 'a needle in the haystack' type of thing. I think we need to stick closer to home. The suspects we've named. The Mandrake property. Randy, you said Rundell is going to show it tomorrow?"

"Yeah, all the interested parties should be there. Three o'clock. Maybe we'll get a chance to look in their cars, over-hear what they say—anything. Any clue. Maybe this Drew guy will show up."

"Maybe we should bring Craig," you suggest.

"Great idea," Randy concurs. "The doctors said he's basi-cally all right. He just needs a pair of crutches. If he'll agree."

"Talk him into it," Tina orders. "We want to see how those people react when they see him."

You look at Jack, who looks at Randy, who nods.
"Done," you declare.

12
THE LAB

You never cut class. But since Candace is here and not your parents, you figure that you'll try it just this once. So, this Thursday afternoon, you slip out before last period and meet Tina and Jack at the bike rack. Randy has already gone home to go with his mother to the hospital, where they'll pick up Craig.

It's a chilly day and the gray clouds have lowered. More rain seems to be in store. You're surprised at how many people are at the Mandrake property. Half of them are probably just here to gawk at the ashes of the mansion. That area is cordoned off by yellow police tape, and two officers stand guard. Investigators are still sifting through the ruins.

It's an eerie sight. The ground is barren, with only a few burned stubs of timber littered in the black and gray ash. But a couple of things remain standing, like soldiers who have refused to surrender. One is the great brick chimney, which rose from the fireplace. The other is a scorched network of naked plumbing pipes, still in place, oblivious to the fact that the rooms, which they once served, have been annihilated.

Aside from the gawkers, the mood of the crowd is grim. At least, most of the crowd. Betsy Akers and Bill Cabot seem to have some "spring in their step". Mr. Rundell hardly glances at the charred ruins, as he strides through the crowd.

Mr. Rundell claps his hands heartily. "Those who are serious about the property," he announces, "please join me in the building over here. Those who are not, please go home."

Rundell leads the way into the barn-like building. It survived the fire, though the wall facing the house is blackened. As you file with the others toward the door, you notice Diane Rivers standing next to Craig. Craig leans on a pair of crutches. Both stare silently at the remains of the mansion. Sorrow and Mordar are doing the same, arm in arm, a few yards away. Somehow you guess cutting classes isn't a new concept for those two.

About fifteen people come into the building. Your eyes widen in surprise, as you enter. It's not a barn at all. It's a single, spacious room. There's one round window high on the front wall, which allows in a shaft of light. Work tables line the walls, some of them strewn with decaying lab apparatuses. And there are drawers, many drawers, on top of the tables, under them, between them.

"This must have been his laboratory," Jack murmurs.

Rundell stands up on a chair to speak. "We all regret the terrible destruction next door," he begins. "Rest assured that if foul play was involved, the police will do their job."

"I can tell you who did it!" Betsy Akers's voice rings out. She thrusts an accusing finger toward the door. At first, you think she's pointing at Tina. Then, you see that Sorrow and Mordar are just entering the room. "Those two! They're the ones who were conducting unspeakable rites in the house."

"Very good." Rundell nods. "You can give the officers outside any information you have when our tour is done."

Sorrow blinks back tears. Mordar draws her close to him. "We didn't start the fire," he protests.

"We'll let the police decide that," Rundell declares. Then, he rubs his hands together. "In the meantime, however, we have business to take care of. The situation of the Mandrake estate has changed considerably. First of all, there is no longer any question of the property being kept as a historical landmark. It ought to be open for development now."

Rundell pauses to survey his audience. "Normally, that would occur by auction," he goes on. "However, this is on hold until we can look into a second matter—which is that prior to the state deadline, Bill Cabot has filed papers, which claim that he has found an heir to the estate. This heir has agreed to sell the property to him."

All eyes go to Bill Cabot. He's bouncing on his toes near Rundell, his cheeks rosy with satisfaction. "Sorry, everyone," he says. He can barely contain his excitement. "But take a good look at the land. It may be the last time you see it in its natural state."

A crisp voice comes from the back. "Your claim will never prove out."

Everyone turns. It's Carlos, wearing a three-piece suit. "If you have evidence, bring it forward," Rundell demands.

"Mr. Cabot's alleged heir is named Peter Mandrake," Carlos answers. "Bill, have you done any research on this fellow?"

"He's told me himself that he's a long-lost cousin," Bill says. He glances at a brown-haired man, about 24, standing beside him. It must be the alleged heir. "Isn't that right?"

"Yes," the man says, his voice cracking a bit. "A few times removed to be sure, but still related by blood."

"Ha!"

This exclamation shocks the crowd. It comes from Betsy.

She hides a giggle behind her hand. "I'm sorry, Bill, but I checked your guy out a long time ago. He's a fraud."

"We'll see about that," Bill mutters indignantly. Peter Mandrake murmurs something into his ear.

Rundell tries to keep his voice upbeat. "All right, we may yet have an auction! On that note, shall we tour the property? I hope everyone brought their walking boots. Anything that you don't want to carry around with you, you can leave on the bench by the door."

People begin to shuffle out, dropping folders, umbrellas, and bags on a long bench beside the door. Craig is standing near the doorway, watching everyone go by.

You pretend to follow the crowd for a moment. But you hang back, then drift back to the door of the lab, where Craig is still standing. The other Digital Detectives do the same.

"Did you recognize anyone?" you ask Craig.

"No, I didn't," he says. "Sorry."

Randy pats him on the arm. "That's all right." He turns to the rest of you. "I'm going to stick with my mom. But this is our chance. Check out Mandrake's lab."

Tina glances at the bench, piled with belongings. "That and a few other things."

"Let's get started," you say. "There's a lot of stuff to check out, and we don't have forever."

DIGITAL DETECTIVES

It's time
for your final
investigation.

http://www.ddmysteries.com

and enter the key phrase

MANDRAKESLAB

When you've finished
this investigation, the
web site will give you
a page number
to return to.

Craig has been acting as a lookout, while you conduct your investigation. When he calls that Rundell and the tour are coming back, you scramble to get everything back in its place. Everything, that is, but the crucial documents, which you've found about Mandrake and his family history.

Rundell's face coils into a scowl when he sees you. "What are you kids doing in here? Haven't you caused enough trouble?"

"No, not nearly enough," Tina replies. "I think that we've found some answers to a lot of questions about the Mandrake property that have been bugging us."

"Answers?" he responds with disdain. "You're under suspicion for any number of crimes relating to this property. I should have you arrested, right now, along with those other two weirdos!"

"Oh yeah?" Tina shoots back. "Why don't you call in those officers standing outside?"

You grab Tina's arm and pull her toward the door. "Just give us a few minutes," you say to the assembled crowd.

Rundell's features have tightened into a grimace. "I've had enough! This will end—"

To your shock, the next voice you hear is Carlos's. "Give them a chance, Rundell. I, for one, would like to hear what they have to say."

"Really, Mr. Rundell," Diane Rivers scolds. "You needn't speak to them that way."

By now, everyone is looking to see how Mr. Rundell will respond. He hesitates, then makes an exaggerated gesture of deference. "Let the juvenile oracles speak."

"We'll be back in five minutes," you promise.

Rundell just waves you out in disgust. He asks the rest of

the audience if they have any questions about the property.

You grab your Jack Pack and step outside the lab with the rest of the Digital Detectives. There you draw your conclusions about the real heir to the Mandrake estate and the fire that burned down the house.

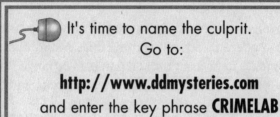

It's time to name the culprit.
Go to:

http://www.ddmysteries.com
and enter the key phrase **CRIMELAB**

Do not read ahead!

While you've been deciding on the culprit, Rundell has brought the two officers standing guard over the remains of the house into the lab. He's ready to have the four of you, along with Sorrow and Mordar, hauled down to the station. So, the answers you've come up with better be good.

Everyone is staring at you, so you start talking fast. "We've made a discovery about Tibias Mandrake," you begin. "That wasn't his real name. He changed it from Tyrone Schmidt. That means that Peter Mandrake isn't actually related to Tibias. He just happens to have the same name."

"That can't be true," Bill Cabot declares.

"But it is," Carlos responds. "I knew Mandrake well. His real name was Schmidt."

"I've checked your guy out, too, Bill," Betsy says with relish. "He's not related to Tibias."

Bill turns to the brown-haired man next to him. "Didn't you say you had documentation?"

"Uh, not really," the guy answers. "I just figured..."

Bill's shoulders droop. He covers his face, which has turned bright red, with his hands. "I can't believe it."

"Pardon me for asking," Rundell breaks in. "But what does this have to do with the fire?"

"Since Mr. Cabot doesn't have a real heir on his side, he needed to burn the house down in order to prevent it from being made into a historic landmark," you explain. "He wanted to win it in the auction."

"That makes no sense," Rundell snaps. "Look at him. He obviously did think he had an heir on his side, right up until one minute ago."

"Uh, that's kind of true," Jack murmurs in your ear. "Cabot has no motive for setting the fire."

You get a horrible sinking feeling in your stomach, as it all becomes clear. Bill isn't the one. You excuse yourself and ask for another five minutes.

Oops! Try naming the culprit
again. Go to:

http://www.ddmysteries.com
and enter the key phrase **CRIMELAB**

While you've been deciding on the culprit, Rundell has brought the two officers standing guard over the remains of the house into the lab. He's ready to have the four of you, along with Sorrow and Mordar, hauled down to the station. So, the answers you've come up with better be good.

"I know who set the Mandrake house on fire," you announce to the room. You turn to Sorrow and Mordar, who are standing near you. "I'm sorry, you guys. But not that sorry. Your luck has run out. It was you."

"You're psycho!" Mordar responds.

"No, that would be you," you reply coolly. "The fire may have been an accident. But I don't think so. You've been terrorizing kids for a week with your chain letter. If they don't forward the letter, you make sure that the curse comes true by making something happen to them—like with Danny's bike."

"A harmless Halloween prank," Mordar says.

"I saw you on the bluff that night," you say to Sorrow.

"I came out with the firemen," she replies triumphantly. "You can ask them. I was so upset about the house that I went out walking along the ocean. That's when you saw me."

Tina jabs you in the ribs. "See? She's got an alibi. I told you it wasn't her!"

Your mistake! Try naming the
culprit again. Go to:
http://www.ddmysteries.com
and enter the key phrase **CRIMELAB**

Outside of Mandrake's lab, you announce that you've made your decision.

"Who do you think?" Tina asks.

You reveal your choice, explain your logic, and wait to see the looks of amazement on the other detectives' faces.

It's not there.

Tina shakes her head first. Then, Randy. Finally, Jack confirms it. "Makes no sense," he says. "You've got to think this through harder."

"Really?" You thought you had it all figured out.

Tina shoves the MicroJack into your hands. "Really. Come on, get back to work. Those people are waiting on us inside."

Go back to the crime lab
and try again!
http://www.ddmysteries.com
and enter the key phrase **CRIMELAB**

While you've been deciding on the culprit, Rundell has brought the two officers standing guard over the remains of the house into the lab. He's ready to have the four of you, along with Sorrow and Mordar, hauled down to the station. So, the answers you've come up with better be good.

You walk to the front of the lab with Tina, Randy, and Jack. Conversation dies down. Everyone stares.

You take a deep breath and begin. "First of all, Tibias Mandrake was not born Tibias Mandrake. He was born Tyrone Schmidt, in Bavaria. He changed his name when he moved to this country. So, even though their last names are the same, Peter Mandrake is not related to Tibias by blood."

You notice Carlos nodding in agreement. "But another name shows up on the family tree," you go on. "Craig Wheeler. His mother was Elizabeth Wheeler. She was the grandniece of Mandrake. His father's name was Wheeler. Craig was given up for a adoption, a few days after birth, and has never known his birth family." You hold up the papers that you found in the safe. "The real heir to the Mandrake estate is Craig Wheeler."

Everyone turns to look. Craig appears stunned. Diane puts a hand on his shoulder.

"So?" Betsy blurts. "Who set the fire? It was probably still those kids."

Tina steps forward. "No. There's only one person who had the motive to set the fire. You, Ms. Akers.

"What?" she shrieks.

"You told Bill Cabot and others that you also had an heir on your side," Randy explains. "But, then suddenly, at the beginning of the week, you didn't. That's because we res-cued Craig from the cave, where Kirk and Drew were keeping him for you."

"I don't know what you're talking about," Betsy claims.

"I think you probably do," you say. "You're the only other one who claimed to have an heir. Craig is the only other heir we know of. He was being held in the house, then the cave. He has to have been your candidate. Especially, since you suddenly went quiet about having an heir, once we rescued him. Kirk and Drew were working for you."

"I told you that I don't know what you're talking about," Betsy repeats. "Anyway, this has nothing to do with the fire."

"But it does," Randy answers. "Unlike Mr. Cabot, you did good research. You knew Peter wasn't actually related to Mandrake, so you didn't have to worry about him. But you knew that my mom still had the best shot at the house, by saving it as a historical landmark. Craig was going to prevent her from doing that."

"You knew that he had never had access to the kind of goodies you were offering," you add. "He was perfectly happy to go along with what Kirk said, so long as the goodies kept coming—for a while."

"Once you lost him," Randy concludes, "you became desperate. You were set on getting the property. You had staked your whole future on it. There was only one way out: destroy the house. Most likely, you had Drew set the fire."

"That's ridiculous," Betsy huffs.

"We've seen the evidence," Tina says. "It's in your briefcase. We know that your secret client doesn't exist. It's yourself."

"So, what if I want to win the auction?" Betsy screams. "I don't know these Kirk and Drew people!"

Carlos speaks up. "I think you do. You have a son, from a marriage that ended years ago, don't you Betsy? And his name is Andrew. Nicknamed Drew. I've been following him. And I wondered why he kept meeting with a big blond surfer."

Diane Rivers is staring at Betsy with wide eyes. "That also explains why you've been dropping all your clients," Diane says slowly. "You cleared the decks because you figured that you'd be set for life by this deal."

"Plus, you've got your plans for a subdivision drawn up already," Jack points out. He nods toward the bench. "It's all in there."

Betsy makes a sudden lunge for her satchel. The two police officers block her way. "We'll take this for you," one of them says, picking up the satchel.

The other takes her elbow. "Come with us, please."

Betsy rips her elbow away and stalks toward the exit. She pauses at the door to burn holes through Craig with her eyes. Then she leaves. The officers rush after her.

Craig watches her go. He turns back to the four of you, blinking back tears.

"That's the only reason they were giving me all that stuff," he says. "They were using me."

Randy puts a hand on his shoulder. "That's true," he says. "I'm sorry."

"But look on the bright side," Jack adds. "You're the new owner of eighty acres of oceanfront land."

13
EMERALD HANDS

A new rainstorm sweeps into town that night. Luckily, you are safely off the bluff and out of its way. You're gathered around a nice warm fire with the Digital Detectives and Randy's mom. Candace is making tacos, and Eve is prancing about the room, in her tiger costume, happy to have it full of people.

Randy's dog Joe is there, too. He trots from person to person, staring at your tacos. Since most of you are sitting on the rug near the fire, he's face to face with you. His pink tongue slurps out in anticipation. He seems to know that tacos are messy, and that every once in a while, some filling will inevitably come dribbling out of the back end of one.

Eve is a special favorite of his, until she pounces on him. "What's the matter, doggie, are you afraid of a kitty cat?" she taunts. Joe races back over to Randy, who gives him a scratch.

"So, does it look like Craig will get the Mandrake estate?" Randy asks his mom. She's just returned from Rundell's office.

"It looks that way," Diane Rivers says. "Once Mr. Rundell took a careful look at those papers you found, Peter Mandrake admitted that he wasn't related to Tibias. Rundell must be a golf player or something. He looked pretty disappointed that Bill Cabot's candidate lost out."

"So, where did this Peter guy come from?" you wonder.

"Reno," Diane says. "He was doing some research on his own name, when he heard about Tibias. I guess he became a sort of groupie of Tibias, but was never able to actually meet him. Bill promised him Tibias's lab, in exchange for making a deal for the rest of the property."

"So, Mr. Cabot just didn't check this guy out?" Jack asks.

Diane shakes her head. "It surprises me. He's usually very thorough. But I guess that he wanted to believe so badly that Peter was his man, that he failed to do his homework."

"Betsy did hers, though," Tina remarks. "As bad as she is, I think she's a lot sharper than Bill."

Randy shakes his head. "I just can't believe that she'd actually keep Craig in that cave for two days."

"You were right that she was desperate," Diane says. "Her entire future was riding on getting the estate. She'd told her clients to get lost, and borrowed and mortgaged up to her eyeballs to win the auction. She's the kind of woman who can't conceive of failure."

Candace arrives with another tray of tacos. Joe stares at it with renewed hope as she sets it on a side table.

"Sometimes, it can be good to have that much drive," Candace comments. "But sometimes, if you lose, you just have to accept that you've lost and do it gracefully."

You smile at her, as you reach for another taco. Candace may not be the best parental figure in the world, but she does have some wisdom. Your parents are coming back tomorrow, and you're starting to feel like you'll miss Candace.

Just then, the doorbell rings. Candace goes to answer. A minute later, Carlos Ramirez enters the room. He gives you all a hearty greeting, and congratulates you on your success.

You make room for him on the stone bench in front of the fire. Candace hands him a plate. Joe immediately trots up and fixes him with pleading eyes.

Carlos looks at each of the four of you. "I have to admit, I thought your group was only going to get in the way. In fact, at one time I suspected *you* of being involved in the fire."

"You're not the only one," Randy says.

"Yes, and that was no accident. Betsy was spreading rumors about both you and that other group—the Shadows. I did some checking around. She was the source of all the rumors from the start. She was quite clever in the way that she manipulated people."

"She must have been good at it," you observe. "She got Kirk and Drew working for her. Through them, I guess, she convinced Craig to go along with her."

Carlos sets his plate down. "She's very shrewd at sizing people up. Most good real estate agents are. She understood that Craig never really had anyone to care for him. He also had little experience of the world, and little taste of life's luxuries. Giving him just a little bit of that, would go a long way. I'm sure that she would have given him quite a nice chunk of money for the property, had her scheme worked. Enough to keep him happy, but still only a fraction of what the estate was worth. The same is true of Drew and Kirk. I'm sure that they were being well-rewarded."

"So, what about this Drew guy?" Tina asks.

"They picked him up just an hour ago," Carlos says. "He's just who I expected—Betsy's son. He was carrying a key that fit the lock mechanism of the mansion door. The lock, of course, didn't burn, and the police kept it as evidence. Once they showed it to Drew, he broke down and told them every-thing. Kirk was a friend of his who he brought in on the deal. Probably, had dreams of going on the surf trip of his life, once he was paid off."

Diane clears her throat. "If you don't mind my asking, Mr. Ramirez—what brought you up here? What made you become involved with the Mandrake estate?"

"Not at all." Carlos pauses to think for a moment. "I was Tibias's lawyer for a number of years, as you may know. I just wanted to see the right thing done with the property. But since I was not formally involved, I felt I should keep a low profile. It seemed to me that you and your group were doing a fine job."

Diane smiles. But, suddenly, her eyes turn wide with alarm. Catching her expression, Carlos jumps to the side. Then he laughs. Joe has just snarfed all the food on his plate.

You begin to apologize, but Carlos just reaches out to pet the Joe. You notice Carlos's ring again. "Did Tibias give you that ring?" you ask.

Carlos holds it up for others to see. "Yes. It's his family crest, as you may know. Well, his invented family crest."

A wistful look comes into his eye. "Tibias was a fascinating character. I visited him at his house many times. I enjoyed his company. He was a full of stories, theories, anecdotes." Carlos chuckles. "Some of which may even have been true."

You all nod, unsure what to say next. Finally, Diane says, "It was nice of you to come."

Carlos stands. "My pleasure. I'm terribly sorry about the loss of the house, as you can imagine."

"We are too," Randy says sympathetically.

"Well, you haven't seen the last of me," Carlos says. "It

appears I have a new client: Craig. He's waiting for me at the hotel right now. I'll be representing him in the transfer of the deed. I'll make sure that he's set up in comfortable circumstances, before I leave."

"We'll help him, too," you promise. "Just tell us what we can do."

"Thank you," Carlos replies. "I'm sure that he'll welcome visitors. He's going to convert the lab into a living space for himself. As for the rest of the property, I believe that he intends to keep it as a nature preserve."

"That's good news," Randy says.

Carlos bows, then shakes each of your hands in turn.

As he takes Tina's hand, you notice an interesting color of green on her fingernails. Uh oh. Is she still hanging around with the Shadows? After Carlos has left, you gaze down at her nails again.

"So Tina, what's the new color called?" you ask, bracing yourself for some gross-out name.

To your relief, she answers, "Emerald."

You grin. It looks as if the Digital Detectives are back to normal. Well, you think, studying the faces of your friends, as normal as we want to be.

ABOUT THE AUTHOR

Jay Montavon lives in San Francisco. He has written more than twenty books and computer games under different pen names, including a number of books in the *Choose Your Own Adventure* series, and the computer games: *Journey into the Brain* and *3D Castle Creator*. He's hard at work on a new *Digital Detectives Mystery*.

The Scent of Crime

Digital Detectives™ Mystery #3

Who's behind the dog disappearances in Crescent Bay?

Randy's cocker spaniel, Joe, is lost. But what gets the Digital Detectives really worried is that a pattern of dog disappearances is beginning to emerge all over Crescent Bay. Is Joe just another victim of this rash of dognappings? And who is behind them? Is it just a matter of rivalry between dog breeders for the upcoming county show or is it part of a plot to continue genetic research on canines?

To solve the mystery, you'll make on-line investigations. Analyze every fingerprint, interrogate every suspect, and record everything in your on-line crime journal. Remember: if you miss a single clue, you might not live to solve another case.

Available soon in bookstores!